THEODORE

XAVIER'S HATCHLINGS BOOK 2

KATHI S. BARTON

This is a work of fiction. Names, characters, places, and incidents are products of the author's imagination or are used fictitiously and are not to be construed as real. Any resemblance to actual events, locations, organizations, or persons, living or dead, is entirely coincidental.

World Castle Publishing, LLC
Pensacola, Florida
Copyright © Kathi S. Barton 2020
Paperback ISBN: 9781953271464
eBook ISBN: 9781953271471
First Edition World Castle Publishing, LLC, December 7, 2020
http://www.worldcastlepublishing.com
Licensing Notes
Cover: Karen Fuller
Editor: Maxine Bringenberg

Prologue

Long ago, at a time when all creatures roamed the earth as only their true self. Working with and helping humans in whatever way they could. Where magic was celebrated. And dragons darkened the skies every day. It was then man figured out there was magic in the dragons and hunted them almost to extinction.

"I'm afraid there is no hope for us." No one made a sound as their leader continued. "Once the humans found out about us and what we can do for them dead, we were doomed. I'm so terribly sorry."

Coop looked around the room. There were so few of them now, he could easily count them. When he had been younger, thousands of years ago, there would not be enough room for all of them to share this cave. Now they were down to a quarter of them sharing the space because so many, his own wife included, had been murdered so needlessly. Coop was saddened by it all.

Turning to leave the large cave, he was stopped by

his brother, Xavier.

"The boys, they are well?" He nodded and smiled. Coop felt it all the way to his heart, a place that had been dead for so long, it seemed. "You have the spell? You are going to use it on them? I so wish I had thought of this before my own family was taken from me, Coop. You are a brave dragon and a good father."

"Thank you. And I shall use it tonight. It is the only way to save them." Xavier nodded his own heart heavy with the losses they had suffered. "You know I would have shared should I have had it sooner. I am so sorry, brother. All of my heart, it's sorry for you."

"I know that. I do. But they are all gone now. My other half, my children. Killed for things not fair to our kind." Coop knew all too well. "Aria was a good woman, Coop. A good dragoness, and mother to your sons. She will be missed forever."

"Aye, in my heart and those of my sons." Xavier stood there for several seconds, and Coop told him he must go. "They're waiting for word on what is to happen with us all."

"One more thing, if you please. It will not take but a second. I have left them all I have. It is where you keep them hidden away, the boys. Deep within the cave, it's all there." Coop asked him what he meant. "I cannot go on, brother. I cannot. There is too much grief in my heart for me to live. I have left my things for them there. They might survive this with the magic you have to give to them. And if so, they'll need more than you have to help them."

"Xavier, please, you mustn't do this. They'll miss you as much as I." Xavier nodded and said it had begun. "You can come and stay with my family. You'll live deep within the caves."

"Nay. I cannot. I must go. Just tell them I love them. With all of my heart." There would be no stopping him once his heart was made up, Coop knew this, but it made his heart no less full for it. "Goodbye, my brother. Take care you are not caught by the humans."

Coop made his way back to his hidden cave and sat before the fire. The boys, he knew, were resting, their bodies getting stronger daily with their age. Soon they would be as big as him, dragons of worth and size.

When his eldest son came to him, his eyes full of fear, Coop knew it was well past time he did what he had been practicing. The magic would keep them safe.

Gathering his sons, six of them of varying shades of blues and greens, he asked them to have a seat. He had a story to tell them. It was not a story, not truly, but a tale that would hopefully keep them safe.

"A witch told me once of a great magic only few can do. It takes a loving heart and a strong dragon to make it work. I have asked her, and she has told me how to make it so. This magic, it will keep you all safe from the humans." They nodded, each of them knowing it was a human blade that took the life of their dear mother. "I will perform this upon you, each of you at the same time, and give you some magic you will use when you need it.

This magic, strong and powerful, will let you roam with the humans, and they'll not know your true self is just below your flesh."

"You mean we'll be humans as well?" He nodded, then shook his head at Cooper, his oldest. "I don't understand, Father. Will you explain?"

"Yes. The magic I will give you will let you change into your true self when you are alone. But when you are out in the world, you will need to be a human. A man." Cooper looked at his brothers, then back at him as he continued. "With this magic, I will also give you a gift. Something you will need to keep yourself safe should they find out. Stronger armor than any other dragon before you, as well as the same immortality you have now, as man or dragon."

Hudson stared at him for long moments. He was the thinker, and if he could think of a reason for this not to work, he would voice it loudly. He was much like his mother in that. She would be the first to say when she did or did not like something and the first to say the plan was perfect. He only hoped she would have approved of this.

"I think you are very smart, Father, to try and keep us safe. But I can only think this will not work on you. Or is that your plan?" The boy was much too smart, Coop thought. "If you change us, who will change you?"

"There will be no one to change me, son. I will.... It is my wish to join your mother in this earth." He watched them, seeing if they understood the love he had lost when she was murdered. "Giving you this magic, it will be something I can tell her I've done for her sons. You know as well as I that she loved you more than anything on this earth, including herself."

"She died saving us." Coop nodded at Lincoln. "I'm not happy you're going to die, Father, but I understand wanting to be with Mother. I miss her more every day."

"As do I." He looked at his sons, all of them growing into dragons of worth. "I must have an agreement from you all. Even if one of you does not want this, it will not work. I would say you should think on this hard. For once I have given this to you, there will be no going back."

"I wish to have it." He knew Cooper would be the first. Not that he did not love his father, but Cooper would see things in a way most would not. To not have this done would mean certain death for them all. Dragons were too valuable dead not to be hunted for all time. "I will do whatever it takes to make sure you are proud of me, as well."

"I am already, Cooper. Forever."

The others nodded too. They were as ready for this as he was dreading it. Because once he started the process to change his sons into men, he would begin to die. It would take all he was to change them.

Standing up, spreading his wings out behind him, Coop told them about the things their uncle had left them. They knew where the family jewels were, the things their mother had left them as well. Once they were standing, their bodies strong and healthy, he felt his heart swell and break for what he was about to do.

"I, Cooper Manning, of the Manning Dragons of the earth, give to my sons, Cooper, Hudson, Lincoln, Lucas, Tristan, and Xavier, all I am. Each of you will take a part of the earth with you when you are converted. The part of you that is unique in all ways will be strengthened and enhanced. You will be immortal, forever, and those you take to your heart will be as well."

His sons bowed before him when he told them to. He said the words over them that would change them to men. Coop could feel his body shutting down, his heart beating a little less. But he had one more thing he wished to bless them with and held himself upright to give it from his own dying heart. "One day, true love will come to you, and you will have more than you have ever known. It will fill you in ways you cannot ever imagine. Love will be yours for all times. For only then will you become a true dragon, a Manning Dragon."

~*~

Cooper sat with his brothers while their father lay dying. His heart was weak from what Coop had done, and it was tearing him apart. Father was weak, yes, but he continued to tell them tales of their mother, of their adventures when they were only small dragons. They were going to be alone soon; their father was so close to joining their mother; it hurt Cooper in ways he had not expected.

"What shall we do with his body?" Cooper looked at Tristan and asked him what he meant. "He will not be able to lie here. If the humans were to find him, they would surely cut him up into pieces. I do not want that for him. We were never able to bury Mother in the proper way after what they did to her."

"We could burn his body." Cooper wondered how it would work when Hudson continued. "His scales will be worthless to them should they come upon his body. The magic he held within him also will be useless to them. He will be nothing more than a carcass they'll leave alone."

Burn his body. It was something to think about. But Coop did not want to, not while he was still breathing, his body still alive. When he laid his head upon his father's chest, hearing his heart beating slower and slower, Cooper wondered what his father would think if he knew the magic he had given them had not worked. They were all still dragons.

"He gave his life to keep us safe. But it did not work." No one said anything to him as they each watched their father. "Dragons such as we are, we'll be hunted and killed by the humans. There is nothing we can do but wait for them."

"We will survive if we stay here." Cooper told Xavier they would have to leave there eventually. "To feed and to fly, yes. But perhaps we could do it only at night. Keep to the skies and not let them see us."

"They know we are about and will have spies out looking for our lairs. We will have to kill any man should he come for us, and still, we will not be safe. We are, after all, dragons who have a great deal of magic."

Coop stopped breathing. Cooper did not hear his father's heart and knew it was at an end. He was quiet for a bit longer, waiting, hoping for just one more beat, one more sound to show he was still alive. But there was nothing. Their father was dead.

Sitting up, Cooper told them their father had passed from this world into the next. None of them had ever seen a dragon die before. Their mother had been dead when they found her. Each dragon they had come upon when they were out had been dead long before they found them, their bodies stripped of every part, so they did not resemble a dragon and were no more than a pile of bones.

Their scales were used for roofs for human homes and for shields. The very meat of them was roasted and stored away so it could be used for medicines and potions. Hearts were cut up and dried, then ground into a powder to use for other things the humans would use to keep them from sickness, as well as magic to have a grand garden and trees heavy with fruit. The only part that would be left was the bones, and sometimes even those were carried off and used for something. Cooper hated all humans.

"We will do as suggested by Hudson. It is the only assured way we can—"

Before he could finish, Cooper felt the stirring of the earth. It shook so hard it knocked each of them off their feet. As they lay there, terrified someone was coming for them, their father appeared before them.

His body was still aground, but instead of being dark in death, he was brilliant in light. Faeries, thousands upon thousands of faeries, seemed to be covering him. Before Cooper could tell them to stop, to leave him alone, Father spoke.

"I love you, my sons." Each of them nodded — fear was almost something Cooper could touch. "I will now and forever join my true love, your mother. I must warn you when you find your other half, and you will, you will have to be careful of the slayers. They will know what you have found by the magic you both will share. My sons, you will leave this place and take your place among men. Becoming someone I will be proud of."

"Father, the magic didn't work. We're still dragons." Cooper felt shameful to say this to his father. To tell him his sacrifice had not worked. "We will be hunted and killed."

"Nay, you only need to think of being your other half. Becoming a man is simple. The same when you wish to be your true self." Cooper was not sure what that meant, but his father continued before he could ask. "Go now, before men come here. The magic to hide me will draw them here. Be safe, my sons, and know I love you more than I do any other creature in this place."

Cooper stood then as the faeries were still working, taking the body of his father apart. But as he watched, he could see they were not doing anything but preserving his body. Faerie ropes were all around him, strings of magic wrapped around him like a cocoon. It made him invisible to all. As Cooper stood there, his brothers beside him, he knew that, like him, they mourned the loss of yet another parent.

"You are the eldest." He nodded to the faerie when she asked. "We have a gift for you. For all of you, but you will receive the most. Your father was a great man, your mother, a queen among her people. We wish to bestow upon you all your father had."

"My brothers, they will need it as well. I should like to share." She smiled at him and bowed. "What have you done with his body?"

"He is being prepared to be moved. We will make a grand garden upon him. Flowers will be there for all to see, but few will know a dragon is there with his other half, his love." He nodded. It was as it should be. "You will take this gift? You will share, but as I said, you will get more than the others."

"I don't care. Please, just do what you must so we can hide." She nodded again and touched her fingers, small, tiny ones, to his forehead. Then she did the same to the others before coming back to him. "It is done. You have shared it with us?"

"I have, Lord Cooper. But you must leave here now. There are humans coming. The magic we used to do this thing has given them cause to come here." He nodded and looked at the ground where their father had been. "He is safe. Just as your mother is now. Go, before they find you here and murder you as well."

He thanked her for her help and left. The exit from

this part of the cave was hidden so well only they knew about it. As they made their way into the night, he thought of the human inside of him, and the pain of it took his breath away. In seconds he was down on his knees. Whatever was happening, he was surely going to die.

"You're a man." He looked up at Hudson as they all began to transfer to men. "We'll be safe now, all of us. We'll be humans for them until we can find a place where we can be ourselves."

"I don't think that's ever going to happen again." Hudson nodded and held his head tightly as he did so. "We will need to train ourselves in their ways. Become what they are. But never monsters."

"No, never."

They made their way to a building; any would do for now. Hudson, like him, was staggering a little, but they were getting stronger as they moved.

Hudson turned to look at him as they were settling in the empty shell of a house. "We will need to buy things, houses and such."

"Yes. But tomorrow. I am too tired to think beyond how much we have lost." Hudson and the others agreed. "When the humans are gone from our cave, we'll go and find what Father was telling us about earlier, about the wealth that will keep us safe."

"I only hope there is a great deal of it. I don't know how to work." Cooper told Xavier, the youngest brother, they would soon learn. "I hope so. I hope so."

Cooper did as well. It was going to be hard enough for them to learn to eat and dress like humans, much less get around. Cooper hoped this worked. For he was as afraid as he had ever been in his life.

~*~

After a time, thousands of years, each of the dragons turned into men, forging their way into a world so different from the one they had been born to it seemed a different planet. But survive they did.

Having their mates come to them, children born to all of them gave them hope—a small and fragile thing after such hardships they were born to. Cooper became, as his father had been before him, the king of dragons—his mate, Carson, their queen. It had been and still was a time for celebration. To this day, they commemorated often and hard at each new birth of the dragons turned men and women.

The others, his brothers, prospered too, finding their other halves, making their magic stronger for having their love. They worked hard in keeping everyone safe and well fed, humans or other dragons. No one, not anyone in need, would ever be turned away from their help. The Manning dragons, true to their father and mother, became the most powerful dragons ever born.

Of the six sons, Xavier's sons, four hatchlings, and two humans moved far away to be the next generation of Manning dragons that would open their hearts and doors for all creatures. Even the sons of their hearts, the two human born men, carried powerful magic. They used it, with their brothers, to help as many people as possible, humans and dragons alike, to live in the ever-changing world. To help them not only succeed but to perhaps help someone else when they needed it. These boys, now men, have stories to tell.

Chapter 1

Patrick got out of the car he'd borrowed and started up toward his mom's house. When the man, a big guy, stepped out from the house, Patrick stopped. They seemed to be eyeing one another when Patrick realized that he had a right to be going into the house because his mom lived there. Walking closer, the man came toward the steps and leaned against the post that he supposed was holding up the porch roof.

"You need something, Patrick?" That startled Patrick, and he stopped again. He was sort of glad for it. He'd gotten himself out of shape in the last few years and needed to rest more and more. "The house and the lands here are being protected by my family until the will is read."

"What the hell does that mean?" The man told him. "I don't want to steal anything—what a thing to say to me. I'm here to pick up a few things my dad said I could have when he passed on. I'll just get them and be on my way."

"What items are they? I can check with Mrs. Black when she gets back to see what he left you." *Damn it,* Patrick thought. Everyone had an angle to keep him from getting some shit from the house. "Do you have them written down?"

"No, I don't have them written down. I'm going into that house, and you're going to get out of my way or else you're going to be hurt." The man looked him up and down before bursting out into peals of laughter. "What the hell do you think is so fucking funny?"

"I would say that it has to do with you trying to tangle with a man that is obviously not only stronger than you'll ever be but fit too." The woman that spoke was behind him, and he turned to look at her. "Hello, Father. I see you're up to your old shit again, aren't you? However, if you're smart at all, which everyone knows you're not, you will just walk away and live to see another day."

"Pembroke?" She nodded at him as she made her way up to the porch where the other man was. "I thought you was dead. What the hell are you doing here now? There ain't a thing here for you."

"And you know this how, I'm wondering? It doesn't matter. I'm here for Grandma." Pem looked at the man, then back at him. "I was wrong to stop you from tangling with this guy. You should do it. It might be the best laugh I've had in a while when he kicks your ass all the way to that piece of shit you're driving around. Isn't that Millie Jackson's car? Did you steal that too?"

"No, I didn't steal it. She lent it to me." The man put

out his hand and told Pem his name. "You didn't offer me the same kind of courtesy, Mr. Manning. Why is that?"

"You're here thinking that you can scam your mom out of her things. She's here because her grandma asked her to be." Mr. George Manning leaned against the post again. "The will can be read now that your daughter is here. Until then, you aren't getting in this house. Even after the will is read, I'm doubting very much that you'll have much in the way of a welcome mat being put out."

Pem asked if she could go inside. After telling his daughter that she could, George told her that her grandma was out to dinner with his brother. Pem went into the house without a word to him. Damn it, why was it that everyone treated him like this? He was a Black, too.

"You should be going, Patrick. I'm sure that if your phone is still working, they'll notify you when the reading will be done. I'm sure even after death, Harold has plenty to say to you and your brother Austin." Patrick asked how he knew so much about his family. "I'm interested in not just who they are, but what their thoughts are, unlike you. You only want to know what sort of things you can get from people. Mrs. Jackson has called the police on you. She's only just found out that you took her car again. I'm assuming you'll be in jail before the end of the day."

Patrick got back in the car and decided he'd be back later tonight. With the old lady in the house with his kid, he was a shoo-in to be able to knock the two of them around enough to get something to tide him over until the will.

He didn't even know what the hell his parents had that they figured needed to be mentioned in a will, of all things. Damn it, the last time he was in the house before his dad died, there hadn't been much more than the four walls and some crap that nobody in their right mind would want.

Taking the car back to Ms. Jackson, he found the police there waiting for him.

"I'm sorry, Ms. Jackson, I surely am. I needed to go and see my mom, and then my daughter showed up. I should have asked, I know." She huffed at him. "No harm done. As soon as my dad's will is read, I'll even put gas in your car for you."

He was thrown against the car and read his rights. The entire time he was trying his best to talk to Ms. Jackson, the old bitch, about not pressing charges against him for just borrowing her car for a bit. As soon as he was put in the back seat of the cruiser, Patrick tried the same thing on the cops.

"It wasn't gone that long. I meant to tell her, but I wanted to see my little girl." The cop turned around and asked if Pem was back in town. "Yes, that's who I'm talking about. She sure did grow up to be a pretty thing. You should be asking her out."

"I'm married. How that kid is a part of you, I'll never understand." He said he had good genes to pass on to her. "You would think you had something to do with her being an upstanding person. How much do you know about Pem, Patrick? I'm betting you don't even have a clue as to not only how old she is, but when her birthday is. Do you?"

"I don't care about such things as age. Besides, if she's older than twenty, then I don't want to know." The cop turned around, saying something about bastard fathers. "I bet you don't know it either, now do you?"

"She's twenty-seven. Her birthday is in December, the same day as mine. She and I went to grade school together. That was about the time she skipped a bunch of grades." The cop turned back to him. "She's also been to war. I'm betting you didn't know that either."

"Why are you drilling me about my kid? Don't you have anything better to do than to tell me shit that I don't give two shits about?" Patrick looked out the window as he continued. "She's here on account'a her thinking she is going to be getting something from my parents. Well, I know whatever they had to give her, it's not worth her coming here to get it."

He had no idea where his daughter had even been living. She'd left his home when she was a teenager. Not that she'd moved all that far away. His mom and dad had taken her in for a little while. At least he thought so. It seemed that every time he went over there, she'd be right up his ass again. It was his dad who had kept him from hitting her.

They more than likely had thrown her to the side of the road too. He'd had enough of her wanting to get into his business. Maggie, her mom, she'd been sick back then too, if he remembered right. All Pem wanted her mom to do was to leave him, and then they'd be all right. How all right did she think they was going to be when Maggie was dying? Whatever the reason, Pem had left home, leaving him to care for her mother. Pem should have been doing right by her mom.

Patrick had spent just one day with his sickly wife before he'd had enough of her whining and wanting him to get her up and around to the bathroom. He called her an ambulance that night after knocking her around a little to shut her up. When they had taken her away, he'd never slept so well as he did that first night. He'd not seen hide nor hair of Maggie or Pem since, except for at Maggie's funeral some weeks later.

He'd only been notified that she'd finally passed on when the funeral place wanted him to pay the bill. Fuck that shit. He had more important matters to attend to than paying for a funeral that he knew damn good and well the state had money for.

Once he was in his jail cell, he was left alone. Patrick liked himself as company. He was the only one that gave himself the answers he wanted to hear. Laughing a little at that, he did wonder when supper would be served. If he remembered rightly, as it hadn't been that long since he'd been locked up, they had a pretty good meal plan going on.

Patrick had been told some days ago that he'd been mentioned in his dad's will. What he could have left him after Patrick had gotten everything out of the house that was worth anything, Patrick didn't know. He'd been taking things from the house since Maggie had died. If not for taking the shit, he'd have had nothing. No food. No house. Nothing but the shirt on his back.

He did think on what the cop had told him about his daughter, Pem. Could she really be twenty-seven? And what was that bullshit about her being in the war? There hadn't been any wars that he'd heard of since his dad had been in one. Thinking of that, Patrick did wonder if Pem had any money. She'd be ripe for picking if she did.

When she'd been no more than about five or so, the doctors wanted her tested. He thought for sure that they were going to see if she was retarded or something. But it turned out they thought she was some kind of gifted kid. Maggie had wanted to put her into some program or another. The only program that Patrick was aware of was one that drunks went to. So, he put his foot down and said to make her go where the rest of them kids went. He didn't know what had happened after that, now that he thought on it. For all he knew and cared about, Pem had disappeared off the face of the earth.

She'd been all right as someone to knock around a little. About the time he'd been told she was gifted, she got right smarter at not being anywhere close enough to him to hit. And that little shit had started carrying a shiv with her — a shiv, of all things. Pem had gotten him good with it a few times too. Not that he wasn't able to get a few licks in himself, but she wasn't any fun after that.

Her being smarter than him didn't help either. Patrick thought for sure that she'd be egging him on when it came to him using words wrong.

"If I say them, then that's the way she should have said them. Kids don't have any respect for their parents anymore." The voice from down the hall had him realizing he wasn't the only one in the jail this time. She told him that nobody treated a person any worse than fucking family. "You got that right."

"What you in here for? Knock over a liquor store? Did you perhaps kill someone? I'm in here for no other reason than the judge told me that without a house or job, I couldn't leave. I have one, damn it." He didn't know if that was all the reason but didn't say anything to her about that.

"No, I didn't kill anyone. I wanted to, let me tell you. But now I have to figure out a way to get out of here and go to the reading of my dad's will. It should have been done sooner, but my daughter was out someplace and couldn't be reached. She's a bitch too." The woman laughed. "I had me the steaks all lined up to steal, but this is putting a damper on things I got going."

She told him she had the same issues. "That son of a bitch even said he was going to sell off my car. How the hell am I supposed to get around and to my job and house if he does that? I'm gonna be telling them who's boss, let me tell you. I have myself a plan, and once I'm out of here, I'm going to be executing it and a few shits that have been doing me wrong too. I'm Sandra Merkle.

I'm going to be a millionaire as soon as someone gets their head out of their ass and figures out that I've been falsely jailed."

He just rolled his eyes and laid back on his bunk. Patrick no more believed she was going to get out than he believed he was going to win the next lottery. Some people, he thought, thinking that they were more than they really were, got on his last nerve.

"Here's your meal, Patrick." He must have fallen asleep and rolled out of the cot onto the floor when the person spoke to him. Christ, he could barely get up off the floor, he was so out of shape. "The doc will be in to see you in the morning. He's making sure you don't have anything likely to make us sick. I mean, other than your stench. When was the last time you had a shower? You smell like rotted meat."

Taking the tray, he stayed on the floor where he'd landed. Even if he had a table, he wasn't sure he would have been able to get up to eat at it. Once he had the covers off the plates, he hollered for the cop again. When he came back, Patrick showed him what was on his plate.

"I know what's there, moron. I'm the one that fixed it up for you. What's wrong with it?" Patrick didn't know where to start, so he just pointed at it again. "Yeah? So? You should be thankful that you're getting anything at all. Eat it and shut up."

"All I got was a bologna sandwich here. Some *baked* chips of some sort. Why would someone bake chips when they can have them deep fried? Where is the mashed taters and gravy? Even a little bit of mayo wouldn't go unnoticed by me. How am I supposed to get enough with this little bit of food? Come on. You're pulling a funny on me, aren't you? Get me one of the meals like you used to bring me: sliced ham and some taters with gravy on it. There was dessert too. Ice cream and pie. This ain't enough for me to get the hunger pangs to go away."

"Oh, sorry. I forgot you were in a five-star hotel and that I should have brought you a wine list too. Will that be all right?" Patrick told him that he'd take a nice bottle of wine if they was offering it. "We're not. You'll eat what you got and be happy for anything at all. We don't have the funds like we used to when there was a cook that would bring by meals."

When the cop walked away, Patrick asked about the wine list. When the door slammed behind the other man, Patrick wondered what the hell the world was coming to. Offering a man a wine list, then taking it away was beyond cruel, he thought.

He picked up the sandwich and bit down into the thing. "One slice of bologna? Where's the mustard and cheese? I like chips on my bologna sandwich too." He ate the dried-out sandwich and looked around for something else. The chips were baked, and he couldn't stand them. He was glad now that he'd not put them on his sandwich like he usually did. "Water to drink? What kind of shitty fucked up place are they running here?"

"They keep telling me that I'm in jail. Like that's supposed to be a good excuse for them not taking the time to cut away the crusts and shit. Christ, don't even bother with the coffee you get. It's like dirty water." Sandra asked him what he'd gotten to eat. "Yeah, got the same thing. It must be Tuesday. That's what you get for dinner on Tuesday. Tomorrow we'll have fish sticks. I don't think they're actually made of fish, but that's only because I'm used to the finer things in meals. When I get out of here, I'm going to be making some major changes in this town."

He let her go on about her money and the things she was going to do. For the first time in longer than he cared to remember, he went to bed hungry. Even when he had no place to call his own, he'd always had a snack or two before hitting the hay. Patrick was going to have to have someone listen to him about the way he was being treated in here.

~*~

Pem hugged her grandma twice before she sat down. The man with her, Theo something, was standing there like someone had to explain to him that he needed to breathe before he passed out. When it finally occurred to him, she thought, he smiled like he'd just learned a new trick.

"Theo and his brothers have been taking good care of me since your grandda passed on. They helped us out too before Harold went and left me behind. He just loved those Manning boys." Pem told her grandma that was nice. "You staying here for a bit, honey? I sure would love to be able to have you around a little more than you've been able to come see me."

"I have no other plans than I've got to see a doctor while I'm here. It's been set up by the hospital where I was until recently." Grandma asked her if she was doing better. "It depends on how you would qualify better. You know what's wrong with me."

"I do." She looked at George, who she'd been enjoying talking to before her Grandma returned. "Pem was in the service for a while. She's a good doctor too. Surgeon, I mean. When she was hurt last year, the president himself gave me a call to tell me that they were taking the best kind of care of her."

"What happened?" Grandma started to answer George, but she said it was up to Pem if she wanted them to know. "I'm sorry. I should mind my own business."

"My unit was dropped off in the middle of nowhere by helicopter about sixteen months ago. It was me and another surgeon and four core men. Instead of it being a drop and go, the chopper we were in was hit by a grenade just as it was going airborne again. It brought it down nearly on top of the six of us. The other surgeon and one of the core men were cut in half by the blades still turning. Another had his head removed. Not that he used it all that much in the first place, but it would have been nice to have his help. I was shot three times, twice in the belly, once in the arm. The third core man was killed even before we were able to retreat to the wooded area where we were headed." No one said a word to tell her that was enough, so for some reason, she continued. Not even the doctors she saw for her mental health knew the next part. "Billy had no idea how to cut into me to get the bullets out, so I had to assist him in the surgery. After he had removed the bullets, he taped me together with some tape that was in the kit he'd brought with him. He ended up wrapping me up with a towel to keep me from bleeding into the man we were there to operate on."

"Where were you?" She didn't answer Theo. "I'm assuming by what you're telling us that you were in country. What else happened that day? There was more, right?"

"Billy kept telling me he'd had enough. Like he was ready to take the next transport out of the place. There wasn't any way we could get out until someone remembered we'd been dropped off. As I operated on a few more men, it occurred to me that I'd had enough as well." She looked at her grandma as she finished what she shouldn't have been telling them in the first place. "It wasn't the first time I tried to kill myself. Nor the last, as you know. My mind was so fucked up by what was going on around me that I couldn't deal with it anymore — any of it. My entire life became a series of blood and pain. I cut into my wrists and decided I didn't want to deal with shit anymore."

"I'm sorry." She turned and looked at Theo. "I've been in similar situations, but never as bad as I'm sure you had it. Being a surgeon or any kind of medical personnel would have been ten times worse than any other soldier. When you think you've been handed just too much for one person to cope with. I served during wartime as well. Not as a surgeon, but as a fighter, and I know how defeated a person can get when nothing seems to stop falling on your head."

"My head doesn't work like most people's." It was George who asked her what she meant. "I've never discussed with anyone before how it works except my grandparents. They never understood it any more than I did. When I'm really stressed, I can see things three or four steps ahead of what I'm doing—like just enough time for me to duck but not get away from what's coming at me. Also, I have an eidetic memory. Once I see or hear something, I can recall it, again and again, to examine and use. It was why I was able to be a doctor, then a surgeon when I was in the service. But with that, I also saw all the blood. Bodies. Even hearing the screams every time I closed my eyes."

"How does that work with your depression?" Theo asked this time, and she told him how she felt. "So, it's too much for your mind and body to be able to retain memories like the one where you were shot. I'm assuming you might even be able to feel the pain too. But you had this before you went into the service. Can I also assume that you have bad memories of living with your parents? And that is what had you trying to end your life?"

"Everything is still there. Every little bit of my life, from having my father drop me several times when I was a baby to the way he smelled when he took my mom's cancer pain drugs to get high. He knocked me around a good deal too. I will take some of the blame for that. I did, on occasion, correct him on things." She smiled, and it felt alien on her face. "If that wasn't enough, I have memories of all the things I did to end my life. The pain of those. The way the water turned pink when I cut my wrists—the feel of the car when it impacted with my body on the street. I couldn't seem to catch a break on things just being quiet, normal. Whatever the fuck that means."

"May I touch you?" Theo didn't move off the couch he'd sat down on when he'd started breathing again. "I promise you, I won't hurt you or touch you with anything more than my finger. I have a bit of magic that I can share with you that might well help you with some quiet that you want."

"People have tried before." He told her that he'd not. "What are you? I mean, you said that you have a bit of magic. I think that's a lie and that you have plenty enough to take my life should you want to."

"I'm a dragon. And I'd never harm you or anyone in your family." She looked at George when he nodded, then at her grandma, who also confirmed that he was telling her the truth. "I do have a great deal of magic. I just didn't want you to.... I don't know that you'd freak out, but I didn't want to startle you into getting more than I want to help you with."

"Why?" He nodded and smiled at her. "You're not as charming as you think you are, Mr. Manning. You tell me why you want to help me when I'm nothing to you."

"You are. You mean a great deal to me, Pem. I'm your mate." He hadn't moved. Not even to touch her. Even from where he was sitting, he could have touched her without her ever thinking a thing about it. "I won't lie to you again about what I can do for you. Touching you will share what I have in the way of magic. I don't know how much you're going to get, but I would like to try and help you as much as I can."

"Why would you assume that I want anything from you at all?" He smiled at her, and she felt her heart flutter. "I think perhaps you should tell me more about what it is you think you can add to my already shitty life by touching me. Right now, all I can think about is that you're out of your gourd for thinking I'd trust anything about you."

"Fair enough." He didn't move back on the couch but did put his hand down. "I'll work on you trusting me if you would do me a favor, and please call me or one of my brothers when you feel the need to end your life again. Not that you can. As of the moment I figured out who you were to me, you became immortal."

"How the fuck did you manage that? You didn't touch me, did you?" He said for her to be safe, all he had to do was to claim her verbally. When she stood up, so did he. "Take it back. Right now, take back whatever mumbo jumbo you used on me to make it so I'd not be able to die."

"I can't." Theo looked at his brother, then back at her. "Your father is in jail. He'll only be there for a limited time — three days. After that, I will be around in the event he tries something else. He's out to get into this house. And he won't stop at anything or anyone to get inside."

"How do you know this?" It was Grandma who told her that her dad had been snooping around since before Harold had passed on. "Did he have something to do with Grandda dying?"

When her grandma didn't answer her, she turned and got down on her knees to ask her again. She had tears in her eyes when she finally looked at her, and Pem hurt for them. He had — she knew it.

"There is really nothing that proves he did." She asked Theo what he knew. "The death of your grandda is listed as suspicious, not as a homicide — not yet, at any rate. But I'm having my mom and my aunts look into things. We don't know for sure that he killed him, but with the way things fell into place, it makes him look guilty as hell. It's one of the reasons that one of my brothers or myself is here with your grandma all the time. I don't think, even if he didn't have anything to do with your grandda's death, he'd not stop at anything to kill your grandmother too if he thought he could make a dime off her."

"He's been sneaking into the house for years. Your grandda and I, we've been putting some things away so we could make sure we had a little to tide us over when we were old enough to stop working. Patrick, he found it and took it all before either of us knew what he was about. I just don't know what I would have done living out here all by myself if these Manning boys hadn't come around when they did. Thanks to them, I have a roof over my head and some money to get by on."

"Thank you." Neither man said anything when she spoke. "What can I do to help you keep my grandma safe? You do know that there is another son, correct? While he likes to put on airs that he's wealthy, I know that Austin is broker than my grandma here. He needs watching too."

"If you tell me their names, I'll have my aunt look into them. She has connections that you'd not believe." George laughed a little at that. "Okay, all of my family has connections. Aunt Carson is more connected than I think most of the world leaders. Including the president."

"I don't know why you're doing this or why you took my grandparents under your wings, but I do appreciate it. Even though I have a father and an uncle, Grandma is all I have." She told him the names of the other two—even the kids. "The kids, Stan and David, are shits. Neither one of them would have lived very long if they'd spoken to me the way they have their parents. They need their asses beaten."

"I'll keep that in mind." Theo put out his hand. "I want to help you, Pem. I need to see that you're going to be all right. I won't push you into anything. But for the sake of your grandma and you, I'd like it if you were to take the magic I have to offer you."

"What will it do to me?" He said other than giving her something that would protect her and a few little things, he didn't know. "I guess that is about all I can expect. But no more. I don't know what this shit is going to be bringing around, but I want to deal with it as best I can. If you show any fear to my family, they'll eat you alive."

"I'm a dragon. I'll be doing the eating if anything goes tits up." She stared at him for several seconds before she laughed again. It was the first time she'd laughed…well, in longer than she could remember. "If you would, just touch my hand, and we'll both be safe."

"How will you be safe?" He told her. "Oh. I guess I never thought about it along those lines. If I'm hurt, you'll kill someone and go to jail. Please don't kill anyone."

She put her hand into his. There wasn't anything at first, just a tingle that started at the tips of her fingers. Then as she stood there, she realized that whatever she was getting, it was powerful as fuck. Trying to pull her hand from his, it was like they were glued together. Pem had a feeling, just as she was falling back that he hadn't any idea at all it that going to be this epic.

Chapter 2

Theo finished cleaning out the gutters as he spoke to his aunt. Aunt Carson was able to find out a great deal about Pem's relatives. Not only were there several warrants out for her dad in different states, but he also was wanted in connection with a few mailbox robberies.

This guy Austin. He's a piece of shit of the highest order. His wife, Caroline, she's someone I would absolutely hate. One of those "my shit doesn't stink" kind of club women. Theo laughed and asked her if she'd found out much about the kids. *Yes. They've been in three boarding schools since they started school. The oldest one, Stanley, is a failure at about anything he does. I don't say that to be mean, but he can't even read. He's twelve years old, for Christ's sake. Right now, they're being homeschooled. I bet that is going over well too.*

Pem told me yesterday that she hadn't seen them in a while. Also, she told me that she's been paying for her grandparents' upkeep since she joined the service. When I asked MaryBeth about it, just to make sure it wasn't stolen out of her mailbox, she told me it went straight into a bank account. Pem made it so no one could take that money out except her grandparents.

I found it. There is just a little over fifty thousand in the account. She really did take care of her grandparents. She also paid for the taxes and repairs around the place. Were you aware that there are about five thousand acres around that place? He told her that Harold told him about it. It was the nest egg that none of them could touch. *Speaking of which, I have some other things you should be made aware of. Pem is a decorated officer. Major in the army. She's been on their payroll since she was hurt overseas. Theo, by all accounts, she should have died over there. The fact that she was able to get away from the chopper makes me think that she's got some magic of her own.*

She told us about that. Theo explained to his aunt what she'd said about being stressed and what she could see. *It could well be magic. But since she has an eidetic memory, it'll be hard not to attach some of what she can see to that. I've seen others with that sort of memory that can do all sorts of things without the benefit of magic.*

I have, as well. Aunt Carson asked him to hang on. As he was coming down the ladder, he saw Grandma sitting in her usual chair out in the grass. He asked her how she was getting along.

"Just fine. It's lovely to have Pem here again. I just wish her grandda had been here to see her too." She looked away, and he didn't comment. "I was thinking that since she's your mate, she should meet the rest of your family. There are a lot of them."

"Yes, there are six of us here, along with our parents,

and I have five uncles, five aunts, as well as a bunch of cousins." She just shook her head. "My mom is going to come out soon with my Aunt Carson. They want to meet Pem, but also Aunt Carson wants to go over some paperwork for the halfway house we're putting together for women getting out of prison who need to be helped to the world again."

"I heard about that. I've yet to go out and see it, but I'm betting it's a humdinger of a place. The newspaper said that it'll be run by the Manning Foundation. That it would be maintained throughout its standing. I'm assuming that means you guys will keep it up." He said that was right. "I feel for those women. Some of them, the paper said, have been in there more than half their lives. I think that would be scary to be released without some kind of help."

"There are things in the place to help us get them trained for jobs too. Computer skills. Their high school education, if that's needed. Most of the legwork has been done for us. The place they were using here in town had all the things listed that they needed. We took that list and put the things that we could into the new building." She told him she was proud of him. "It wasn't my idea, but I thank you for that."

Pem came out of the house just as he was moving the ladder. She did look better today. Rested, at least. When she stretched and yawned, he made himself turn away and go up the ladder again. Christ, she was beautiful.

"I've just heard from the attorney that he's going

to make plans for us to meet at the jail. He told me he thought it would go better if we didn't allow Dad to be freed long enough to go to his office. I told him I liked that idea, but that if you had any qualms about it, I'd call him back." MaryBeth said she liked that idea as well. "Also, Austin and his family are in town. I guess they're staying at the little hotel not far from here."

"Did he bring his family?" She said that he had. "Great. Now I have to make sure that I'm not sitting next to them. I know it sounds horrible to say that about one's grandchildren, but they aren't the grandchildren that I wanted. Mean little shits."

Theo laughed as he pulled the last of the leaves out of the gutter. Tomorrow someone was coming out to put guards on them, so it wouldn't be necessary for this to be done again. Harold used to do it, and Theo had been terrified for him.

"Theo, I wanted to ask you if you'd come with us tomorrow." Theo told Pem that he'd be there. "I don't know what is going to happen, or if anything will. I want my grandma safe, and I have a feeling she won't be if they find out about a few things she and I have set up."

"I'd be glad to be there for the two of you." Pem nodded. "My mom and Aunt Carson will be arriving tonight. Not just to meet you, but to bring some paperwork that we have to go over with the foundation."

"I'm not ready to meet parents yet, Theo. I know that yesterday I might have given you the impression I'm all right with this, but I'm not." She looked worried for a moment before continuing. "Your family, they're well connected, you said. I'm assuming they've looked into my life?"

"Yes." He decided he'd tell her if she asked, but not before then. She was stressing again, and he could almost taste it in the air around her. "Finn and his wife, Rachel, are hoping you and MaryBeth will join us at their home with the rest of my family. Nothing formal, but we do have a lot to talk about with the new building."

"I have to have a lie down, I think." MaryBeth got up from her chair and made her way to Pem. "Honey, don't push him away too much. He's a good boy and has a good heart. You and me, we might wonder someday why we even thought of not being a part of all this."

Pem sat down in her grandma's chair and watched him. Theo let her, wondering what she thought of him but afraid to ask. When she let out a long sigh, he asked her if there was anything he could help her with.

"No. I'm fine just the way I am." He nodded and sat down on the porch steps. "I slept all night. Not a single dream that I can remember. Also, I was thinking of getting dressed, and this is what appeared on my body. I'm assuming that is one of the little things you were talking about. Someone should be warned about something like that, don't you think?"

"I had an idea you'd be able to dress with a thought. But if you remember, I told you I wasn't sure of what you'd get. I am glad to hear you slept well. You look refreshed. Which I'm thinking you're going to need when you take on your family tomorrow." She nodded. "Have you discovered anything else?"

"It's weird, so you tell me if it's something you've never heard of. I can turn down the images in my head. Not turn them down, but off, I guess. I know they're still there, lurking in the background to jump up and put me under again. However, it's like I have some control over it." He told her he didn't know what she might be able to do with her mind. "I thought so. Is it weird?"

"Weird? No, I don't think so. I think it's more of a defense mechanism than weird. It's to help you, and that's what you needed more than anything else, right?" Pem nodded. "There are a couple more things I'd like to talk to you about. If you're ready for it."

"So long as it's not too much. But I guess you'd not know what I think of as too much yet, would you? Just tell me." He put out his hand, and she stared at it. "If you think I'm going to touch you again, you're insane. Once was enough for that shit."

He knew the precise moment she saw the faerie when it landed in his hand. "This is Bubble. They get to pick their own names when they're deemed powerful enough to work with a dragon or his mate. In this case, Bubble will be your faerie. All dragons have one. Mine is Rose. She's here on my shoulder."

"Oh, Theo, he's wonderful." When Bubble realized she was happy with him, he went to stand on her outstretched palm. "My goodness, you're very handsome too. I don't know what you and I can do together, but it will be fun having you nearby, I think."

"Yes, mistress. I will be with you at all times. Not the bathroom or shower. It has been explained to me that you might not be comfortable with someone in the bathroom with you." She laughed, and Theo felt his heart fill with the sound. "I'm here to do your bidding. Whatever it might be, I can do it for you. If you have a thought to change up something, like a wall or anything like that, I can get a crew together and fix it right away."

Pem looked at Theo. "I don't know what to say." He asked her what she meant. "This is the first gift someone has given me in longer than I can remember. Thank you for him. Bubble and I will get along nicely, I think."

"Good. Now, there is one more thing I would like for you to try. This is important on a lot of levels, but it was something that Rachel got when she was mated to my brother Finn. I want you to put out your hand and —"

"What are you? I mean, I understand that you're a dragon, but I know nothing more than that. George told me he wasn't a dragon, but he had all the magic of one. He also told me that Finn is a red dragon. One that can melt even the hardest of material." He told her what he was. "Pearl? I don't know what that is either, I guess."

"I can shift for you. There is more than enough room for me to do it here." She nodded, then shook her head. "What do you want me to do, Pem? Like Bubble, I'm yours to command."

"You're very large, aren't you?" He said he was and left it at that. "I'd love to see your dragon, but I don't want anyone to notice this huge dragon or whatever you might turn into in Grandma's yard."

"No one but you will see me." He moved out into the yard, excited to be able to do this for her. "Be careful of my tail. While my dragon won't mean to harm you, it's large, and he forgets sometimes." She nodded.

Shifting from himself to dragon was like being reborn to him. It wasn't painful, not at all, but he became whole. Every cut or scratch he'd gotten while being a man would simply heal and disappear. His body felt like he'd been given a thorough cleaning, a shower like none other. Theo was very careful when Pem came closer to him.

~*~

Pem didn't know what she had expected when he became the dragon, but he was much larger than she'd thought he'd be. When she was close enough to touch him, Bubble cautioned her to be careful of his spikes.

"They're very sharp, my lady, and since you're so much smaller than they are, they could slice through you without a second warning." She told Bubble she was careful. "He's a pearl dragon, mistress. Only you can see him because of you being his mate. I can because we're together. But he is blended into the grass and trees around him so that no one could see him if he was right in front of them."

She could see it then. The way that when he took a breath, the trees in the yard would shift and change. Pem put out her hand and touched his snout. He was warm, not hot, but she thought he could get hotter when necessary.

"When I was a child, I always thought of a dragon that would rescue me from my family. One that would pick me up and carry me away when it was too much for me. And now, here you are." Theo asked her, in her mind, if she'd like to take a ride. "Can I? I mean, can you — how would that even work?"

Theo put out his clawed hand, and she was startled that just one of his great sharp claws was bigger than she was. Stepping into the middle of his paw, she held on tightly to his finger. They were airborne in seconds. Pem couldn't have dreamed anything like this. Never in her wildest dreams could she have ever thought she'd one day really be riding on a dragon.

The wind on her face was wonderful. Pulling the holder out of her hair, she left it to blow too. There were all kinds of things to see from this height. Pem had never thought the town was so spread out as it was. From this height, too, she was able to see the tops of houses, some of them in terrible repair.

Pem saw yards that had children playing in them without any toys. She knew she should be thinking of the beauty of the things she was seeing. But all Pem could see was how much more the Manning Foundation could be doing in simple things for the older generation. When they landed atop a mountain, she was careful getting off his hand. Her mind was buzzing with things she wanted to say to him.

Wait. Nodding, she watched his face as he seemed

to be listening to someone. *My Aunt Carson is telling me something we both should be aware of. She wants to know if she can connect with you.*

"I suppose. What does she have to do?" The woman was laughing when Pem felt her inside her head. *Well, I guess that question is answered. I'm Pem.*

Yes, child, I know. I have a couple of things that you need to be aware of before you go into this meeting tomorrow. Nothing you can't handle, I'm sure, but you should be made aware of it. If you don't mind, I've invited the others, your new brothers-in-law, Rachel, and Theo, to listen too. Theo nodded, then there were other voices of people she didn't know. Each of them told her their name. *All right, we're all here. Tomorrow I want you to be on your guard with the people in the jail with you. One of them that has been talking to your dad is Sandra Merkle. She's trouble of the worst kind. That isn't what I wanted to tell you, but something you should be told about. I'll leave that up to you, Rachel.*

I can do that. There was a short discussion about Sandra's trial coming up and how they couldn't wait for her to be another name in the books. *Also, I've yet to meet you, Pem, but I'm sure we're going to get along well. Will you be coming to dinner at our house tonight?*

Yes. She looked at Theo, who sat down next to her in the grass. *I can wait to meet you all, however. I'm not sure what you expect, but don't expect too much.*

You're going to fit in perfectly. Now, we need to talk about tomorrow. She could tell that Carson was a hard ass, but it seemed to her that she had a sense of humor too. *While*

I'm not going to be in the room with you when the will is read, I've already broken into the camera system at the jail — particularly the room you will be using. So, don't be surprised if I speak to you.

Do you expect trouble? Carson told her she always did and that Pem more than likely did as well with her training. *Yes, well, if someone pulls out a knife to kill someone, I can sew them back together. That's about as far as my training goes, I'm afraid.*

That will be useful. However, I think you have a great many skills you can pull out as well. I've read the reports, the real ones, of the trouble you ran into that got you shot.

Pem didn't know what to say to that but did look at Theo. When she got up to go and sit closer to him, he wrapped her into his arms and set her on his lap. Pem thought at first, she was going to fight him about taking over like this, but it was about the most comfortable place she could have been right now.

All right. Your grandma carries a gun, did you know that? Pem told Carson she did. *Don't let her take it tomorrow. First, it's against the law. But for some reason, I don't know yet, it is going to be important she's not carrying. I don't know why — sometimes I only get bits and pieces of what is going to happen.*

After twenty minutes of Carson telling them what she knew was going to happen tomorrow, she cautioned them about not letting their guard down. She also said, several times to Theo, to remain calm. While Pem didn't know why that was so important, Theo promised her he'd do his best.

The connection was closed when Carson told them she'd see them tonight. Neither she nor Theo moved to go back home, so she just looked around where they were. It was a beautiful place up here. She thought she would come here a lot if she could fly.

"Are you all right?" She nodded at Theo when he finally spoke. "I'm worried more than I was before about tomorrow. If something gets out of hand, I'd very much like it if you were to cover your grandma, if need be, with your body. I'll have you, but I don't want anything to happen to her either."

"I will gladly do that." She watched his face. "There is more that you're not telling me, isn't there? Something you need for me to know, but you don't want me to freak out. Right?"

"Pretty much. One thing I've been thinking of for the last few days. I want you to hear me out before you agree or disagree. I have a home. It's huge. My family bought each of us one when we moved here. I would like for you and your grandma to come there to live. I won't push you into anything, but I would feel much better if you were someplace safer than you are." She told him yes. "I'm sorry. Yes, to what?"

"I've seen, thanks to you, how far we are from the next home. Also, the police station is further away than I'd like to think about should we need them in a hurry. Last night when I was taking a shower, the hot water went out three times. I know they've been living here all their adult lives, but after my family took what they had, there wasn't enough to fix things when they broke down. I don't think the house is worth more than it would cost to fix it up. I might be wrong, but it's not a sound house either." He told her it wasn't. Even the foundation was falling in. "Yes, I saw that when I had to go down and turn the breaker back on. What will happen to this place once we move out?"

"There are several members of the pack that we can have roaming the yard to keep people out. That's not a big deal. But I think at some point, someone is going to have to make the decision if they want to keep paying taxes on this place or just turn it back to farmland." She asked him what he'd do. "Burn the house out and to the ground. Not by me, but with the fire department in charge. They could use it as a training house. Or we can fix it up enough that you could rent it out should you need the income. Which you don't. We have more than enough money that neither of us would have to work again and would still be able to spend a great deal daily and not make a dent."

"I have to work." He told her he understood that need as well. "Then there's the land. What would you do if it belonged to you? I'm sure you've thought of that."

"Yes. There are several options there. The one that might make your grandma feel the best is where she sells it outright to someone — my family would purchase it — and let us use it for the new hospital this area needs." Standing up, she looked down at the town below her while Theo continued speaking. "We've been working to find enough room to build since we moved here. On the land, there would be a hospital, a clinic, some office buildings, as well as a few homes. With the amount the land is worth, your grandma could feel as if she were helping the town rather than just leaving the only home she's ever known."

"I'm so happy that we don't have to wait until the will is read tomorrow." He said he knew that. "The only thing I can think of right now is that, by selling the land, Grandma would be a target of my family. I don't want her hurt."

"I've not told her yet, but she's immortal as well. I've given her enough magic, however, that if she wishes to join Harold, she can do that as well." She looked at him with a cocked brow. "I gave it to you as well. You could end your life should you really want to. But I'd like it if you gave me a chance first in making you happy. Or at least not as depressed as I know you've been."

"I've never been happy, not until the last few days. I'd have a moment or two of some feeling, but nothing like I've had with you." She looked back down at the town. "I'm not in love with you, Theo. I don't know that I know that feeling. But I do feel something profound for you. And you have made me feel so much better that I've not had to take my medication since arriving here."

"You've no idea how good that makes me feel." She nodded. "Pem, one more thing. You can say no to it if you wish, but this is serious business. I would very much like it if you were to marry me. Today, if possible. Not only will it make you safer when it comes to your family, but they will have me to reckon with if they get the least bit out of line. It would also make it so that you can distance yourself from them. Manning is a name that opens doors. But it can also be counted on to slam the fucker shut should it need to."

"All right." He laughed, and she turned back to him. "Did you expect me to say no? Or were you hoping that?"

"No. I'm thrilled. Mom will be too when they arrive." She nodded, then jokingly asked him if he had a ring. "I do, as a matter of fact. My dad gave it to me when they were here for Finn's marriage."

When he pulled out a small leather sack, she was almost afraid to see what it would look like. Pem wasn't one to want diamonds or big rings. But she thought that if she were able to pick out what she wanted in an engagement ring, it would be emeralds. They were her favorite gem.

"My mom, as I told you, can see bits and pieces of the future. Most of my family can do that. Also, she and my dad have a direct contact with the dead. It's come in handy more times than I think she likes to admit. She said this would make the woman I fell in love with sparkle like this does when the sun is shining on it." The ring was an emerald. She turned to him when he moved to her on his knees. "Pembroke Black Manning, will you be my wife? Keep me safe? Protect me from myself? In turn, I will pamper you, love you, and make sure you come first in all things. As you do now."

"Oh, Theo." The ring slid onto her finger as if it had been measured for just her. The emerald was as big as a nickel and surrounded by several smaller diamonds. The weight of it wasn't heavy, as she thought it would be, but felt like it had been made for her. "Yes. I'll marry you. Anytime. You certainly know how to make a woman swoon, don't you? I love this. Thank you so much for it."

As he shifted and took them down the mountain, she wished that she'd kissed him. Pem had a feeling it would be something more than just a kiss between two people, but a claiming of sorts between the two of them. As soon as they landed in the yard, Grandma came out of the house. Showing her the ring was like having it put on her finger once again. Grandma hugged them both before telling them they needed to get going. The tears in her grandma's eyes made her hug her tighter.

"You look so good together as a couple. I cannot believe how lucky we are to have such a man in our lives." Pem agreed with her. "Oh child, he's going to keep us safe. I just know it."

She had to take a few minutes to gather herself. Pem had always had her emotions take her under at times, but this was nothing like that. She was happy. She felt better than she had in years. Pem only hoped that Theo would not rush her. There was just too much going on for her to deal with a pushy man.

Chapter 3

MaryBeth wasn't sure what the holdup was, but she figured they had a good reason for making them wait for so long. They'd been asked to show up at the jail at nine. They'd been a little early and had been in town since eight, which had afforded them time to have a nice breakfast with the Manning family again. They were leaving to go back home. MaryBeth was going to miss them.

Thinking about the dinner she'd had with Theo's family last night made her smile. Such good people. People that she was glad to be a part of. There was plenty enough food, that was for sure, and the conversation was loud and fun. MaryBeth thought she might have had more fun at that dinner than she'd had at any Thanksgiving with her own family. Yes, she thought, they were nice people.

Theo's mom, Cindi, was such a wonderful person. She was older than her, by a great deal as it turned out, but she looked like she could have been Theo's sister rather than mother. She also told her that she could and did speak to the dead and help them with some things that might have been left undone. Xavier, Theo's father, did as well.

MaryBeth thought of her having all those boys at one time while growing up. But not a one of them were disrespectful to anyone. They were polite and even helped with dinner preparation and clean up without being asked.

When they began talking about the trial, Carson came to sit with her and Pem.

"Two things that I want you to know about tomorrow. I've already asked that neither of you carry into the jail tomorrow. They'll check you and ask, but things have been known to get by even the best of places. Also, after the will is read, try very hard not to engage with your dad. He's off his noodle if you ask me and doesn't deserve anyone being nice to him. I'm sorry to say that, but it's true." MaryBeth had told her that was all right. She knew it as well. "Good. He's going to be getting out the day after tomorrow. There are a few things I can tell you that I know for sure, but they can wait until later. We're going to be leaving as soon as we can in the morning to get back home. You two take care of yourself. Please?"

Now here they were, waiting for Patrick to be brought into the room with them. She looked over at her grandsons. The two of them hadn't acknowledged her at all, not a hug or even a look in her directions when she'd said hello to them. Stanley came to stand in front of her, almost as if he realized she was thinking of him.

"I want some money. Dad said you'd have some." MaryBeth told him that wasn't the way to ask for something. "Like I care. Give me some money so I can get me a pop to drink. Now."

"I will not." He jerked her purse from her, and she took it back. "What do you think you're doing? You do not take my purse."

Before she could put her purse behind her on the seat so he couldn't get to it, he jerked it from her once again. This time he not only broke the strap, but he emptied the contents on the table where it had been. All she could think about was that had she had her gun with her, he might well have found it.

"What the fuck is wrong with you?" Pem jerked the purse from Stanley, put the things back in it, and did put it behind her. "Go back over there and—"

The slap to Pem's face startled MaryBeth as much as it looked like it had Pem. Pem slapped the boy back, not only hard enough to leave a mark on his face, but he was knocked to the floor as well. The look he gave his aunt was enough to make her glad she'd not hit him as she'd wanted to. The child was evil. A terrible thing to say, but he was.

"What the hell do you think you're doing hitting my child?" Caroline snatched up Stanley while he still glared at them. When she looked at Stanley, the red mark on his face was turning purplish even as his mother continued. "I'll have your butt for this, Pem. See if I don't. We don't hit our children. We talk calmly to them and discuss what sort of behavior we condone or not."

"That little fucker needs his ass beat. I don't care for talking like that's going to solve something when he takes things that don't belong to him." Pem looked at her. "Are you all right, Grandma? Did he hurt you?"

"Just scared me." She looked at Theo as he stood behind them. "Honey, something is wrong with your husband. Look at him."

All she did was reach out and touch her hand to his. The calmness that came over Theo was immediate and profound. Shaking himself, as if he were shaking off bad memories, he said he was all right now. Pem asked Theo if he was sure.

"Yes, I'm sure." He leaned closer to her. "You have more strength than you did before, love. You might well have hit him with that. Not that I'm complaining, but just letting you know that the next time it comes to slapping the piss out of him, you should put more of your new powers behind it. That kid is going to be trouble."

Patrick was brought in about then. He looked around the room as if he was looking for someone, then sat down. He looked over at her and nodded but didn't speak to her, his own mother. MaryBeth didn't bother asking him how he was either. The sooner they were able to get out of this place, the better she'd feel.

"Mrs. Black, I'm going to have to ask you to take your children out of here. There isn't any reason for them to be witness to this, and I think they've caused enough trouble for one day." The attorney for them, William Kasen, looked at her and smiled. "I'm sure you all wish to get this over with."

"My children go where we are. If she'd not hit him, then things would have been just fine. I'm going to press charges before we leave here. Pem abused my son." Mr. Kasen rolled his eyes. "You think this is some sort of joke?"

"No, I don't. But since I've been in here, those boys of yours have broken the water fountain, torn the shade down from the window, and pulled out my paperwork, so I had to redo it all. The two of you have sat there like nothing was going on. I don't know where you got your parenting skills, and usually, I'm not one to judge, but they're not good kids. Now, you are more than welcome to go out with them. Your name isn't mentioned in this will reading either. You either leave with them, or I have them escorted out by these fine officers here." Caroline was torn. MaryBeth could see that. She'd very much like it if she left with the kids. But in the end, she decided to stay. "Very good. Now. I'm here to read the last will and testament of Harold Brook Black."

MaryBeth knew what was in the will. Her will said basically the same as his in that they had left the same things to the same people. She only wished that Harold hadn't had to die for her to have to deal with this. The love the two of them shared wasn't like the marriages she'd witnessed by other people.

Last night Pem had married Theo Manning. It hadn't

been much more than them signing the paperwork to make it legal. Theo had put Pem on all his properties and credit that morning, and he'd even given MaryBeth a credit card with her name on it. MaryBeth didn't know what she'd do with such a thing, but it was nice to have the security of knowing it was there.

She looked at Pem when she quietly said her name. "Grandma, he's asking you if you're all right." She said she was. She was musing. It made Pem smile. "I'm so glad to see you happy. You've no idea how happy that makes me."

"Of course, she's happy. What the heck was Dad thinking in leaving her all that land? It's not like she's going to farm it or anything." She was glad to see that leaving Pem everything had upset Austin. "I'm going to contest this will, so don't go getting all settled in that place. It should have come to me. Not you."

"I've already sold it, as of last night. So, it's a moot point now." Austin and Patrick asked her what she was talking about. "The land that the house sits on. The acres that we bought long before you two were born. I sold it to the Manning Foundation yesterday. I'm glad for it too. I'm a very wealthy woman."

"Good, then you're going to be the one that I get money from. Like I pointed out, it should have been mine in the first place. I'll have you know that you're going to be out on your butt, Mom, just as soon as I find an attorney that is willing to do this. Not that I think any of them wouldn't want to take on a case this large, but I want it." MaryBeth just stared at her son. "Oh, come on now. You can't really believe that Patrick and I shouldn't have gotten anything from the estate. You and Dad had to think this was a bad idea to leave everything to Pem. What sort of things did he expect my children to have if not the money?"

"Frankly, Austin, I don't think you have a leg to stand on, but you go on and try suing the Mannings for the land. Theo and his family made me a very generous offer, and I took it. I did speak to Mr. Kasen about it, and he said that since Pem is listed as the sole heir in both of our wills, and she agreed to the sale, then I could do whatever I wanted with it. So, I did." Austin told her what he'd told Pem, not to get too comfortable. "Why, thank you for caring, but I am very comfortable with where I am now. I'm living with Pem and her new husband, Theo."

"Oh, so that's how they took advantage of an old woman without the sense that God gave a rock. They bamboozled you." Austin laughed, and she felt her temper rise up. Old woman indeed. "That'll make things so much easier for me when I take them to court. That money will soon be in my bank account, and the land will be as well."

"What about me?" Austin looked down his nose at his younger brother. "I should get some of that money too. I'm his son as much as you are."

"Yes, but you can't afford an attorney, while I, dear brother, can." Austin laughed again, and when Theo joined him, Austin stopped laughing. "What do you find so funny, Mr. Manning? The fact that I'm smarter than you? Or is it because you just realized that you attached your horse to a broken-down piece of crap woman and a girl that doesn't know enough to get in out of the rain?"

"You are certainly one for turning a phrase, aren't you? And the respect that you pay your mother is astonishing. I'm going to let you in on a few things while we're finishing up here. One, your mother is a smart woman. Smarter than I think you'll ever be. Pem is a billionaire. Yes, you heard me right, billion. She had millions even before she...how did you put it? Oh, attached me to a person who doesn't know to get out of the rain. Well, this is what you might like to call a storm of all storms raining down on your head. Not only do I have more money than you do since you're running on an empty account right now, but I have a great deal of power to back it up with. Money power is the best thing ever, don't you think?" MaryBeth watched both her sons as Theo continued. "The property and the house are sold. As of an hour ago, the house has been torn down, and construction has started on the new hospital. If you're interested to know, it's going to be called the Harold and MaryBeth Black Memorial. Also, this is something you should heed right away. You ever talk to my wife and grandmother like that again, I will not just ruin you, but I will kill you as well."

If Austin was going to say something back to Theo, he was stopped by the officer coming into the room. He looked at them all, now standing, and asked to speak to Theo. Before she could ask the younger man what had happened, the door behind Theo was closed. A uniformed officer was now standing in front of the door, blocking anyone from following. Sitting down, she was terrified out of her mind, thinking of all the things that could have happened. Pem took her hand into hers and told her that Theo would tell her when he knew something.

~*~

"Theo, this is bad. Really bad." Theo, his mind centered on the two people in the room upstairs, nodded. "We didn't have any idea he was carrying. Who would have, I ask you?"

"I don't know. But just remain calm when you talk to them. This isn't going to go well, no matter who was at fault. I'm not saying it was you, but you have to remain calm, or that will go badly for the department. All right?" Captain Amos Shiller nodded and took in and let out two more breaths. "Are you ready to go in and talk to them? I'm going to talk to my wife and her grandmother while you—"

"No. Don't leave me." Theo just looked at him. "I'm sorry. But I don't want to tell them on my own. I need you to be there with me for moral support. This is bad. Really bad."

If he said that to him once more, he was going to knock his block off. This was bad. Any idiot could see it was a fucking mess. As they entered the room where his new family was, he went right to Pem and held her hand.

He'd not been able to tell her anything through their link. He just didn't know what to say. Captain Shiller asked them all to have a seat.

"We've had an incident downstairs in the bullpen — where the officers meet up for the day and the detectives get their notes gathered." Theo cleared his throat. "Yes. All right. Officer Gray, one of my veteran men, was showing your sons around the office. They were headed back to the cells when a man was brought into the station. He was a little wild, and Officer Gray shielded the two boys with his body."

"Good for him. If you expect me to be sorry if he was hurt doing that, you're going to be disappointed. That's his job, after all." Pem told Caroline to shut up. "I will not. I should have known something like this would happen. This is the worst town I've ever been in."

"There's more." They all looked at the captain. "As he was shielding them from the man, Stanley — he's the oldest, I'm to understand — drew a weapon from the back of his shirt and fired two shots at Officer Gray, killing him. Three other officers were shot too. When it was realized that Stanley was the one firing at them, two more officers tried to talk him into putting the gun down. When Stanley fired, killing another officer, they had no choice but to fire back."

"Oh my god. No. You shot my son? He is only a little boy. Is he on his way to the hospital? He'd better be getting the best of care. And I'm not paying for it either. To think that you had me —"

"Shut the hell up and listen to him." Theo looked at Amos. "Go ahead. Tell them the rest. You're doing fine."

Nodding, Amos looked at the couple in front of him. "When Stanley went down, we thought it was over. We were heartbroken for sure, but then David picked up the gun and began firing the rest of the clip at anyone he saw. He was as calm as his brother had been. Firing the gun as if he'd had plenty of practice at firing a weapon." Caroline stood up, and Amos told her to sit down. She did so. "Do you by chance own a gun? Either of you?"

"We both do. And we can discuss how my sons got hold of a gun from one of your men after I go and make sure they're all right." Amos laid the gun, in an evidence bag, between them. "That's my wife's gun. Where did you get it?"

"Stanley had it on his person. There is also a second clip that we took from him. Have you, either of you, taken your sons to an armory? To learn how to shoot a gun?" Caroline answered this time. "You know that there is a reason it's against the law for children to be taught how to fire a gun. They're too young to know that dead is dead. And paying off someone, as you put it, to let them get into such a place will get them shut down as well. My goodness, do you have any idea what sort of mess this has caused? I have five bodies in my station house now that I have to blame directly on the two of you."

"I want to see my sons. Neither of them had better be hurt too badly, or I'm going to own this town."

Caroline stood up and was let out of the room. Austin

followed her. Amos looked at the three of them as Patrick was taken back to his cell. The idiot was laughing the entire time.

"They're both dead." MaryBeth looked at him and put her hand over her mouth in shock. "Stanley drew first and was killed when he fired back at one of the officers that was talking to him. David was killed the same way after he killed another officer and a bystander. Seven others were hurt in all the fire."

"He would have used my gun." Theo told MaryBeth to not say a word. "No. No, I won't. But she knew this might happen. Something would happen. When he took my purse, and it emptied, all I could think about was that I was so glad I'd done what was asked of me."

"Yes. I told you, however, that she can only see bits and pieces. She was talking to me while I was down with the others. Aunt Carson said now that it is over, she can see the chain of events fully. Had you had your gun on you when he took your purse, he would have killed all of us. Or at least tried. Even his little brother. Then he turned the gun on himself, she told me. Had he used your gun, MaryBeth, you would have been guilty of aiding and abetting. Aunt Carson is coming back here with my family to help with the clean up of this. I'm so very sorry for their deaths."

Theo saw that Amos was talking to William. There was going to be big fallout from this. They might even try to make it sound as if William had set the boys up because he'd told them to leave the room. Amos was telling him, in greater detail, what had happened. Pem asked if they could go and see to her uncle and aunt.

There was wailing going on as soon as the elevator doors opened. Theo heard it as soon as they stepped into the elevator, but he'd not mentioned it. Both Caroline and Austin were being held back from touching either of the boys, which wasn't going well. One of the many officers still there said if they didn't behave, he was going to jail them until the forensic officers were done with their job. That didn't shut them up, but it did have them standing back.

"What should we do?" He told Pem he didn't know that any of them could do anything. Not yet, anyway. "They're just little boys, Theo. What would have made them do such a thing as fire on officers?"

Theo, honey, I have them both here with me. Your cousins have found their way to me and are here demanding answers. He asked his mom if she was all right. *Yes, dear, I'm all right. Shaken, as you can well imagine. How are Pem and her lovely grandmother? They're not hurt, are they?*

No. They're taking it as hard as you can imagine. Austin and his wife are throwing around lawsuit threats, but nothing that I'd not expect. What are they saying? If you can tell me. She told him she wanted to speak to Pem as well. *All right. But be gentle with her, Mom. She's hurt by this too.*

Theo held onto Pem as his mom asked her if she was all right. After telling her that she was more worried about her grandma, she told her what she'd told him. That Stanley and David were with her.

Stanley is pissed that he'd not been able to kill his grandma when he had the gun. I'm telling you what they're saying to me. I want you to know I'm not one to sugar coat things. Is that all right? Pem said she'd not have it any other way. *Good girl. I'd not tell your grandmother much of what I relay to you. Please don't. I think it would break her heart more.*

It would, I think. Tell me why he wanted to kill my grandma. Mom told them both what Stanley had told her. *I don't understand. What was his problem with having her around when he rarely saw her?*

He said she was a drain on society. I believe they might well have heard that from their parents. David is talking to me now. He said it's unfair that Stanley got to kill more people than he did. Their plan was to trade off the gun for each of them to have the same amount of kills. Pem looked up at Theo as his mom continued. *They thought they'd not be killed because people would underestimate them and fob them off. Well, Stanley is saying that they bet no one does that again.*

Do they know they're dead? Theo told Pem when she asked him what he meant by that. *Sometimes the dead just think they're hurt or that nothing happened to them. When that happens, they have to figure out what happened to them before Mom or Dad can help them.*

I don't believe Stanley is aware yet. However, David is. Or he's figuring it out on his own. I don't know if you've seen the bodies yet, but David was shot several times in the chest, one of them in the heart, and Stanley was shot three times. One of the bullets hit him in the head. He was dead before he fell over. Pem started crying softly. *I'm so sorry, Pem. I should have thought about that before speaking.*

No. It's all right. I need to know before I see them. Not that knowing it will make it any better, but this will help.

Theo held onto both women as they cried softly. Caroline was finally able to hold her boys, and she pulled them into her arms, sobbing loudly. He was sure he might well have been doing the same had they been his children. *They planned this, didn't they? They planned to come here and make a name for themselves at great cost to a lot of people?*

Yes. Mom told him that they'd be landing soon, and the jet was going back for his dad and the rest of the family. They'd be there until the funerals were over, to support Pem and MaryBeth. When Pem said she was going to take her grandma outside, Mom spoke to him again. *Theo, I don't have to tell you to keep an eye on them. Especially Pem. She's going to take this harder later when it hits her that they're both gone.*

I promise you, I will. There will be a lot of lawsuits from this, I'm thinking." Mom told him that he could count on it. *"I'm assuming too that Aunt Carson has a recording of everything that went down today. She might well need to use them when this goes to trial. I have no idea why, but I have a feeling that somehow, Pem and I are going to be sued over this too.*

I'd say that's a good bet. I'm having Carson find you a good attorney. I'll give you a name when she has one for the two of you." She was quiet for a moment. *Stanley has figured out that he's gone. He's actually threatening me for not sending him back. The boy has some big balls for one so young. I'll give him that. Before I send them on, because I'm sure they're going to cause trouble in the world of the dead, I'll talk to Pem about seeing them. She more than likely won't, but I want her to make that decision.*

Mom told him they were landing now and would be at his house shortly, and he told her how much he loved her. After telling him that she loved him as well, the connection was closed. As he was going to find Pem and her Grandma to take them home, Amos asked him if he'd hang out for a bit.

"The Feds are coming here. Since I have so many officers dead, they've been notified." Theo told him that was a good idea. "I just don't understand this, Theo. Those boys just killed several officers and looked like they might well have killed more had we not taken action and fired back. It's going to be hard on Officer Meadow too. He's the one that killed the younger boy. He kept telling me while they checked his wounds that he has a son that age. I've sent him on to the hospital. He'd not even realized that he'd been shot too."

"I'm thinking you should have every officer here write out what happened. Not only that, but I'd take any recordings you have of this and put them in a locked safe in the bank or someplace. Take a witness with you as you remove the recordings and take them to the bank. Chains of evidence will be your friend in all this." Nodding, Amos asked him if there was more. "Yes. By all means, make sure that no one talks about this to the press, their spouses, or anyone. This gets out, and there will be hell to pay. You know that."

The ambulances arrived to take the boys out of the station house. Austin was too quiet, and Theo suggested that Amos have someone without a gun, travel and stay with him. Amos agreed he'd do that. Theo said to make sure that they took pictures of the places where the bodies had been too, for no reason other than to make sure they recorded everything.

Theo was finally able to leave the station house. His brothers were going to be at his home when they arrived. Not just for support, but to be there to fend off reporters as well as calls. Theo just wanted to hold the two people he'd come to love very much and shut out the world.

He knew he'd not be able to do that. People would want answers. They'd want details. More than anything, they'd want to know what the fuck would make two kids kill and be killed like they were. While he had answers to those questions, he didn't think they would go over well. Theo thought the blame lay squarely on the parents. Who the hell took young kids to a firing range to show them how to fire a gun? He supposed that would come out in the end as well.

Pem was making arrangements to feed everyone after Theo let his family know what was going on. Bubble told him he'd keep a very close eye on his mistress after Theo told him that his family was coming. He'd been with her the entire time, but he was still shocked to hear that both little boys had planned this.

"The older lady will need a faerie soon, your lordship. I should have thought of it sooner." He said he'd not thought of it either. "I'll find her someone that can be calming. Especially now, she doesn't need a flitter bitter around her."

"I don't know what a flitter bitter is, but I'm sure you're right." Bubble smiled. "You take care of my family, Bubble, and I'll be greatly indebted to you."

"'Tis my pleasure, sir."

When Bubble left him, Finn pulled him into his arms and hugged him tightly. It was something he'd not known he needed until just then. Theo felt his eyes fill with tears as his brother told him that he had him. That he loved him. It was perhaps the best news he'd had all day.

Chapter 4

Pem sat on the couch and thought about everything that had happened today. She couldn't block it out any longer. She had to think this through, or it was going to drive her crazy. It was already depressing the fuck out of her. Looking up when she heard her name, she smiled at Cindi. Her mother-in-law was one of a kind and the only other woman she depended on other than her grandma.

"I have a bit of news for you. You can tell me to go the hell away, and I'll do it. It's not terribly important, but just things that I believe that you should know." Pem leaned back on the couch and regarded Cindi. "Are you all right? You don't seem as stressed as I thought you'd be. And to be honest with you, I think you're not nearly as depressed about this as I was afraid. Are you all right?"

"I don't know if you're aware of this or not, but you have the greatest sons that have ever been born." Cindi thanked her. "Theo and his brothers have been pampering me since I got home. Not one of them has left me alone, either. Not until I came in here. You and Xavier should be very proud of yourselves."

"One can only hope we do a good job when raising our children. When they leave home, you hope you've taught them well enough, but let them have enough confidence in themselves, so they make good sound decisions too." Cindi smiled at her. "Thank you for that. You have no idea how wonderful you've made me feel just now."

"I was being honest. And on that note, I'd like for you to be honest with me, even if you think it will hurt me. I love your sons, all of them. But I'm about to put my foot up one of their asses if they don't back the fuck off and stop handling me. So, tell me what it is I need to know. Not what you think I should know. All right?" She nodded and smiled at her. "What's going on?"

"Your cousins are with us. They're here now to tell you what happened the day they were killed. After this, I'm going to send them to the white room. I should explain to you what that is. It's a place where there is no color, no people. Not a sound is heard—not their breathing, foot falls, or anything else. They can walk for miles and not get out of the white of it all. It's a place I send the dead to when they cause trouble." Pem asked her if they were causing trouble there as well. "Yes."

It was enough, she supposed. They'd be sent on, but for now, she could ask them about why they'd done such a thing. Why had they decided that killing others in a police station would have gotten them anything but dead?

"Before I talk to them — and I do want to — would you please tell me what the cops found when they went to their home? I've asked, and I keep getting fobbed off." Cindi said she'd be honest with her on that as well. "I would hope you'd be honest with me even if it is bad."

"It's bad. The boys, from what we can tell, thought they'd live through what happened. There were stashes of money throughout the house, mostly in their rooms. Also, there were several insurance policies they'd taken out. The police have told Cooper it was the most well laid out plan they'd ever witnessed. Them being as young as they were, he said he feared for the world in general for their expertise as they got older. They had planned this action since they found out their grandfather had died. One of them got ahold of the plans for the police station the night before they left, so they knew the layout of the building." Cindi asked her if she was sure she wanted to hear more. Telling her to go on, Pem had a terrible feeling she wasn't going to like what she said to her next. "They assumed — I don't know why — but they assumed that your grandma would have her gun with her. Stanley was going to take her gun and kill MaryBeth. Then he was going to leave the rest of the murders in the room to David. Using the gun, he would get into the station house and was going to go down to the bullpen and kill every person he came in contact with. Neither of them figured they'd be killed as, they've told me, they were kids, and no one would want to hurt them."

She looked in the direction Cindi did. Pem had no

idea what kind of person it took to see the dead, but her respect for her had gone up a few notches. When she looked at her again, Pem got up and went to sit with her. Taking her hand into hers, she looked at the other woman.

"I want to hear it all. But I have a couple of questions. They just popped into my head." Cindi said she'd answer them if she could. "Where are their bodies? Are they going to be buried here or back home where they lived? Also, I'd very much like to do something for the families of the victims. Something to help them along with this. I know that nothing will take the pain away, but I need to help them."

"Each officer has had their funeral paid for. The families will also receive a one-time payment of two-hundred-and-fifty-thousand dollars. It will be funneled through the police department as an on-duty insurance policy. The houses they lived in are being paid off to help the families. The injured officers will not receive a bill from the hospital, and their families are given hotel rooms to be close to their loved ones while they stay in the hospital. They will get their full pay while they're off, as well as a bonus. I'm not sure how much that is going to be. The details are still being worked out." Pem asked her if they could afford that. "Yes. We've been around for a great many years, Pem. We're also mated to dragons. The story behind them being able to cry gems is very true."

She thought about the generosity of this family and

wondered if they had had to do this before. Help a group of people out what had been devasted by someone with a chip on their shoulders. Looking in the direction she thought the boys were, Pem told Cindi she was ready for the rest.

"They've killed before. The two of them. Not with guns, but with knives. I've helped in finding the two little boys they killed, and I've also had Carson look into the four children that were bullied by them that had moved to another school. This wasn't something they did on the spur of the moment. They planned everything. They were, as you might have guessed, monsters." She asked Cindi if Austin or Caroline knew. "Not about the deaths, but they did about the other children being bullied. The entire family had been blocked from every restaurant and every other business in town before they left. It's the reason they're broke, paying off people their children have hurt. And there are a great many of them."

She sat there, thinking of that when she told Cindi she was ready to see the boys. Ready or not, she supposed, Pem wanted to see what they had to say for themselves. Before she was able to see them, Theo came in and sat across from her. Cindi said he was there for support, not to take over.

As soon as they came into focus, she had to turn away for a second. They were dead, bloodied too. After taking a deep breath, she looked at the two of them. Both of them were smiling and looking like they were happy. The little fuckers were proud of themselves, she thought.

"You killed those men. Five men for no reason at all." Theo said it was seven now. One of them died on the operating table that morning, and Amos had had a stroke that they were blaming on the boys. "Did you hear that? You've killed seven people for no fucking reason other than you could."

"Yeah? You would have been one of them too if you'd not talked the old bitch into leaving her gun at home. Christ, you're as bad a fuck up as Dad always says you are." She looked at Theo when he didn't so much as move. "What do you want, Pembroke? We are looking for a way to have some fun here. But this bitch behind you is keeping us under lock and key. That won't work for us. We're kids and need to have some fun, even if she won't fix it so we can be alive. Did they tell you that we have a list of people we're going to take care of? It's huge, and you're on the top of it."

"Why?" He shrugged. David just laughed. The two of them looked like they'd been on the set of a horror movie and hadn't changed out of their gory clothing. "You don't have a reason to want me dead? Well, I guess it sucks for you that you're going to miss that opportunity. You couldn't have killed me anyway. I'm not ever going to die. However, you two are—"

"Everyone dies, dumbass." She looked at David. Such a strong voice for someone that hadn't even begun to shave yet. "You will die, and we're going to be here waiting on you too. Such plans we have for you. Dad and Mom? Them too. They hated you. Did you know that?

Because you think you're so special when you're nothing but a lazy bitch that can't even hold down a job. You're nothing at all like us."

"You have that right. I'm alive, while you two aren't. By the way, have you heard of the white room?" She saw Theo smile, then he laughed. The look on the boys' faces told her they'd heard of it. "That's where you're headed. Right now, as a matter of fact. No mommy. No daddy around. Not even the two of you together anymore. Mom, would you please send these two monsters on their way?"

They didn't just disappear as she thought they would, but actually left behind a cloud of smoke. She looked at Cindi, thanking her for what she'd done for her. Then she looked at Theo. He was still smiling at her even as Cindi left the two of them alone in the room.

"Did you know?" He shook his head. "Take me someplace with your dragon, Theo. Then make love to me. I need to know that we're real. That we're forever. Take me anywhere your dragon wishes."

Taking her by her hand, he took them into the yard. Before she could ask him again to take her, he was his large dragon. Getting into his hand, she held onto him again as he took them to the skies. Whatever happened now, she thought, was something that both of them needed.

~*~

Theo took her to a place he knew better than his own home. The cave he'd been born in. The place where his family had stashed away a great deal of their fortune. He shifted to his other self even as he landed on the soft grass in front of the opening.

Putting his hand on the large stone, he used his magic to move it to the side. Once they were in the cave, he could also light it up with more magic. Today, he wanted to show Pem everything. Then he was going to do as she asked. Make love to her.

"This is wonderful." He let her look around, touching things that hadn't felt the touch of anyone but his family in centuries. "There is so much here. I guess when you're around forever, you can stockpile a lot of stuff."

"Mostly, it's my parents' things in here. And my uncles'. I was told once that I also had a Great Uncle Xavier—my dad was named for him. He lost his wife and children during the great purge. The night they were changed, my dad and his brothers, Great Uncle Xavier, ended his own life because his pain was so great for his loss. He left them what he had accumulated. It's here as well." He watched her pick through some of the gems. There was old money there as well. "Whatever you want from here, we can take it to the house. I guess someplace in here are some furniture pieces as well."

Pem turned and looked at him. She didn't move, so he stayed where he was as well. "You've seen so much. I would imagine that your father has as well. To be around for so long, I can't imagine how much he would have gone through. How much has changed over the centuries."

"Being the youngest, my dad didn't remember much

about his mom. She was murdered by the same people that had killed a lot of other dragons. And you have to remember that before he was changed, his family had been nothing but dragons. Great ones, but they couldn't hide like their sons became able to." He took a few steps toward her. "Dad would tell us how they'd had to learn to walk. Eat with utensils. Even to dress in the clothing of humans. It was as if they were starting over. Learning everything they had to know in order to blend in with the others."

"Are you going to make love to me, Theo?" He said that he was. "I'm not afraid of you. I think that I was. Before you showed me your dragon, I think that I was for a little while. Now I know not only that you won't hurt me, but that you'll keep me safe as well. I've fallen in love with you."

"I love you, as well. Take off your clothing, Pem. I want to see you here, among the gems and stones of my kind. I want to see every inch of you." She was naked before he finished speaking. With a wave of his hand, a bed appeared, covered in warm blankets and silky sheets. "I've thought about bringing you here since I met you. Now all I can think about is making love to you here."

She looked at the bed and moved toward it. He followed her, stripping off his own clothing by hand. If he were to take her now, he knew that not only would he hurt her, but he'd not last long enough for her to have any sort of enjoyment before he did.

Once she was on the bed, he stood over her. Pulling

her legs to the edge, she sat up enough to look at him. Watching her face, seeing her eyes darken, made what he was going to do to her all the more amazing. Licking her, tasting her creaminess made him moan loudly.

"Please. I need to come. Right now." He suckled her clit into his mouth, nipping at the swollen bud. When she screamed, the primal part of him wanted to make her scream again.

She tasted of honey and cream. Her body wrapped around his, her legs tight around his shoulders, Theo feasted on her. Every time she came, screaming her releases, his mouth would fill with her juices. Sliding his fingers into her sheath, Theo paused when she tightened around him so much he couldn't move in and out of her.

Theo lost count of how many times she came for him. Her body was limp until she came, and he thought it the most wonderful thing he'd seen. Crawling up her body, he nipped at her skin. Swirling his tongue in her navel, his nip at her hips. She was so responsive that he felt like a very lucky man. To have her here, beneath him, Theo knew that forever, he would think of her just this way.

Theo removed the last of his clothing. Taking her nipple into his mouth, he suckled hard on the tip. Her hands pulled him closer as he took more of her breast into his mouth. Christ, he could die right now and consider himself a happy man. Death by sex had never been something he believed in until this very moment.

Poised at her entrance, his cock aching now, he told her that he loved her. Filling her, pushing his cock deep within her, Theo came hard enough that he felt his eyes roll to the back of his head. But he was far from finished. His need to come with her, to be one with her, had him taking her as slowly as he could.

Pem touched him everywhere she could reach. His back, his shoulders. When she wrapped her legs around his, holding herself for him, her nails dug deeply into his back. Some part of him knew he was taking her too hard, that he was hurting her. But as soon as she stiffened beneath him, Theo felt his dragon roar at him, moving over him in a way that he was sure he'd enjoyed their mate as much as Theo had.

Dropping on top of her, Theo had to concentrate on breathing. In and out, he told his lungs. In and out. When Pem giggled, he lifted his head up just enough to rest it on her forehead before asking what she'd done to him. The little laugh had him rolling to his side.

"You're hilarious." Looking at her with one eye closed, he couldn't speak as yet. "Did you know that after you come, and it was fucking amazing, that you make little sounds in the back of your throat? A clicking sound."

"That would have been my dragon. That's his sound—like a purr, I guess you could call it." Pem rolled to her side so that she could look at him. "I felt him there. Did you?"

"Yes. He spoke to me too. Telling me that he loved me."

Theo wasn't surprised by that. He told her he loved

her as well. "I saw you talking to my mom earlier. I hate to bring her up at this moment, but did she give you information on being the mate to a dragon?"

"She did." Pem rolled to her back and didn't speak for several moments. "She said that she didn't know if we'd be able to have children. I think that hurt her as much as it did me. She so wants a grandchild. But she did tell me that there any number of children we can adopt, and they'd be just as much ours as if we'd created them ourselves."

"I would love any child you were willing to have with me. By any means. I love you so very much." She told him she did him as well. "There are other things you'll need to know. I should have pointed this out before we came up here. You'll need to eat more red meat, just to be able to keep up with me. It's not just sex, but even when we sleep together. I'm hot all the time, and your body will work on trying to cool you off. Juice too. Anything fresh you want to drink is better than nothing."

"I think our cook told me that this morning. I was still in overwhelmed mode then." He asked her if she was all right now. "I don't think I'll ever be all right. But I think I'm handling things a little better than before. I told you I stopped taking the medication. I've not had to resort to it again at all. I'm proud of me for that. Also, the thought of ending my life hasn't entered my head either. For which I'm very grateful."

"I am too. I nearly forgot to tell you. You had a phone call yesterday from a doctor by the name of Pinchester.

He wants you to call him back about the case against Doctor Charles Shivas. I didn't ask, but I'm assuming he did something to you?" Theo knew what he'd done. Aunt Carson had told him. But he wasn't going to tell Pem that. "Do I need to kill someone for you?"

"No, not yet, at any rate. He tried to get me to sleep with him when I was coming here. I sued him and his practice for it. I have the recordings of everything, and they're telling me they don't have them. Like I'm going to send them the ones I have." He asked her if Carson could look into it. "She already is. She's sort of scary, isn't she?"

"You have no idea. But I'm glad she's doing this. Hell will be paid, and I won't have to see you through bars." He closed his eyes for a moment, just to think about the rest of the things she needed to be told. "Your dad is getting out of jail tomorrow. I'm not sure why they've held him for this long. There is a rumor that he's planning on going to the house to live there. He seems to think you've been lying to him, or someone has, about the place being torn down."

"He'll figure it out."

Theo watched her. She was closing her eyes slower and slower. When she finally fell asleep, he didn't move from his position on the bed. Reaching out to Finn, he told him where he was.

While we're here, is there anything I can bring down for you? Not right away, but tonight sometime. He didn't ask him why he was there, but Theo suspected he might already have figured it out. He asked him if he could find the necklace he'd made for Mom long ago. *Yes. I can find it. I actually think I know just where it is.*

Getting up, careful not to wake Pem, he started toward the area he was looking for. Finn started speaking to him even as he bent to pick up the jewel cases he'd been looking for.

The boys' bodies are being shipped home. Aunt Carson took care that a funeral director from their town was on the plane with them when they left a little while ago. Neither Austin nor Caroline is aware that the boys are riding with them. I thought it was better that way. Theo agreed with him. *He's also going to try and talk them into a graveside service without anything in the paper. It's all over the news about them already. Aunt Carson made sure he understood there were going to be a lot of pissed off people if they had anything more than that. Apparently, the town they live in isn't all that keen on the boys or their parents. I still have trouble wrapping my mind around the things they said to Mom.*

Pem and her grandma are taking it a good deal better than I thought they would. I think MaryBeth is still thinking about leaving her gun at home, and what more could have been done if she'd brought it. I doubt very much they would have let her in with it. He told Finn he'd found the necklace. *How did they get the one gun in? I never thought to ask.*

I saw the recording. Stanley went through the metal detector first, and of course, set off the alarms. While he was emptying his pockets, David put up a hell of a fuss about the toys that he said belonged to him. The two of them were in and out of the detector several times, setting it off. By the time it was settled between them, Stanley just walked into the station while his brother came through with the gun in his back pocket. You can even see when Stanley gave him a thumbs up when they were both on the other side. Christ, to know how smart they were at this is fucking scary. Theo agreed with him. *I think I told you that Amos passed away, didn't I?*

Yes. The guy was stressed to the limit when I spoke to him right afterwards. They're attaching that to the body count too. The state is suing their parents. They said they were negligent by letting them use a firearm in the first place. Not to mention not having the guns locked up away from them. I have a feeling they'd have gotten them anyway. Like you said, they were just too smart. Theo looked around for other things he could bring home for Pem to wear or just to put into the house.

I'm supposed to tell you that you did a fantastic job of taking over the crime scene. The Feds were thrilled to death that you'd had Amos put the recordings and other things in the safe. He said he'd had this happen before. *Yes, but locking the recordings in the safety deposit box 'was a stroke of brilliance. That way, when they arrived, they knew that no one had tampered with anything in it. Even having each of the officers there to write up in their own words, what went down was great.* Theo said he was just making sure everything was where it needed to be. *Speaking of which, I wish you'd think of taking the job as police chief. I know we have a great deal to handle as it is. Having someone right there that can tell us when and where there is trouble would go a long way in us being able to get help to people faster. Think about it. All right?*

I'll talk to Pem. Right now, I want to get to know my wife better. Theo laughed as he sat down on one of the many chairs that were stashed in here. *I don't know how anyone that has been around as long as we have can ever get used to saying that word. Do you know what I mean?*

I do, and you're right. He felt his brother's distraction. *I don't know how much longer you're going to be there, but when you get back, come see me. Nothing terrible, but there have been some developments in the hospital that is going to be built.*

Theo wandered around for a little while longer in the cave. He wasn't really looking for anything but did manage to find a pile of things he wanted to take back with him. One of them was the photo album that their parents had put together when he and his brothers had been born. Even Rachel might get a kick out of seeing them as young dragons.

"What are you doing? I thought I'd broken you." He laughed and handed Pem the album. Sitting up, she dressed, and he was disappointed. He also knew she was sore. He was himself just a little. "Even when you guys were babies, you were huge, weren't you?"

"Finn was bigger because he was hatched first. You'll have to have Mom and Dad tell you about some of the pictures. I'd actually forgotten it was in here. I have some things I'd like for you to wear. With nothing else." Pem looked at him, her eyes so beautiful they took his breath away. "I love you so much, Pem. I don't think if I said that to you every minute, you'd understand the amount of love that I have for you."

"Oh Theo, that was so wonderful." He helped her up and noticed again that she was sore. "I might need to take a long hot bath when we get back."

Feeling both sorry and terrific that he'd made his mate walk with a limp, he wasn't going to tell her that it had taken him twenty minutes to work the kinks out of his own body. Thankfully, he healed quickly, or he was sure he'd never live down how much pain he'd been in from making love with his mate.

Chapter 5

There were news reporters all over the high school, inside and out as it turned out. MaryBeth wanted to tell them all to go to hell. However, she wasn't going to make a scene. Not today. She knew that these people, vultures she thought of them, needed to make a living as much as the next person. Even if it was to go to a funeral for the wonderful souls that had given their lives all in one day.

"Thank you for sitting with me, MaryBeth. I just don't know how I would have functioned if you'd not been here today." Telling her it was her pleasure, MaryBeth felt her eyes fill with tears again. The woman sitting next to her was Linda Benson. Her husband of three years was one of the last murdered by her grandsons. Linda was going to have a baby soon, and that bothered MaryBeth more than anything. That the little boy or girl would never know their father.

The services were all being held in the high school gym. The caskets, all covered in draped flags, were lined up in the gym in front of the chairs. They, too, were lined up tightly on the floor for all the townspeople to be there for the fallen ones' families. Even the bleachers were filled to capacity. The injured officers, as well as the families of the victims, were in the first four rows. The rest of the seats on the floor were for dignitaries, as well as the Mannings — all of them were there.

MaryBeth had never met a family like the Mannings. They weren't just what a person would call close — they were even closer than that. Good to each other too. And she noticed that when one of them went a step too far in joking around, it would only take a look from someone, and they'd bow their head and say how very sorry they were. MaryBeth could hang around them for the rest of her life if they'd allow her to.

Not only were they generous with their money and understanding with each other, but they were also compassionate with everyone they came in contact with. She'd seen Cooper slip some money to a teenager. Milo held a small child while a mother was crying. Each and every one of them had a specialness about them that she wished more people had with each other.

When the service was over, she helped Linda up from her chair. As they walked past all the other caskets, she waited with her as she paused by her husband's. That was when a movement out of the corner of her eye had her pulling the younger woman closer to her. The microphone nearly hit the two of them in the face.

"We were wondering how you felt about your grandchildren." MaryBeth, having had enough of that question slapping her in the face, knocked the microphone from the man's hand and grabbed him by the tie.

"How do I feel about my grandchildren? That's the question you have for us right now? You should be ashamed of yourself. I bet your mother is right proud of her son. Coming up on a grieving widow to ask someone that sort of question. Have you no heart, young man? Don't you care that there are seven dead family members right here in front of you?" She knew she was causing a scene, something she'd not wanted to do, but it was high time, MaryBeth thought. "A better question would have been to ask the families *'Do you need anything?'* Without that contraption in your hand too. Do you know this woman's name? The name of her poor husband? She lost everything the other day. Not a one of you came here to do anything but get a story. Well, let me give you one. Linda Benson lost her husband of three years the other day. Yes, it was my grandsons that did it. I hurt for all these people on a level that you obviously cannot understand. Mrs. Shiller lost her husband of thirty-nine years. He was set to retire, and now he's gone as well. Mr. Lance over there, he has five little boys that he's now going to have to raise all on his own. Did you think to ask him if he needed something? Perhaps you could have kept an eye on his boys while he grieved on his own for a moment? No, you wanted to shove that thing in my face for a story that will sell you papers or have people tune into your newscast. There are any number of people here that would have asked a better question than how I felt.

You want to know? Well, here you go. I'm hurt—all the way through my heart. I'm confused. What would make little boys want to murder? I hurt for my son and his wife. My niece and her new husband. I hurt for this town and the grief that has hit them as hard as it could have. Look at you standing there with that thing in your hand, your recorder out, so you don't miss a thing." MaryBeth started crying, with no hope of stopping the tears now. "In a few weeks, less I'm betting, you're going to be on to another story—another big one—and this town and the people here will be nothing more than a note—not even a noteworthy reminder will be on your recorder—while the people here will still be reeling from the deaths. Dealing with the day to day things, like having to remember that their loved ones are not going to be coming through the door. Not being there to take the children to the store or to get ice cream. Young man, you should be ashamed of yourself and what you've come here to do. Leave us alone, why don't you?"

She walked out of the gym, holding tightly onto Linda. When they were at the car, she got in with the younger woman when she begged her to. Turning to her, she told her how sorry she was.

Linda smiled at her. "I'm not sorry. And you shouldn't be either. My husband would have been so proud of you. He would have laughed his ass off too. You gave me a little of him just then. Telling them vultures off. That's what he called them. So, I thank you for that, MaryBeth. Those people will just go on and label you as a crazy woman. But there will be a few here today that will say, 'There goes MaryBeth. You should have seen her taking a bite out of one of them idiots.' Thank you."

There was to be a gathering at the home of Finn and his wife. MaryBeth hadn't planned on going. It was just too much for her to go on pretending she wasn't dying inside for what her family had done to this town. But Cindi had asked her to come along, and she didn't think it was right, for all they'd done for her, to turn them down.

There was enough food for the entire town being set up. MaryBeth hadn't had much of an appetite for the last few days. All she could think about was how Stanley had looked at her and Pem. Even in the middle of the night, she'd see his eyes staring at her, and she just couldn't shake the feeling that had she brought her gun with her, he would have tried to kill her.

Of course, her reasonable mind told her she didn't have to worry about that. There wasn't much of a chance she'd have gotten it inside. But her mind and heart just couldn't deal with it. None of it, as a matter of fact.

"Grandma?" She smiled at Pem. "Are you all right? You look a little lost. Come on into the kitchen with me. The women are in there making tea and talking. I think they're also eating. My goodness, they sure can put the food away. And not gain an ounce."

"I'm not hungry." She went with Pem into the kitchen and heard them laughing as soon as she entered. It wasn't as if she didn't want anyone to laugh, but MaryBeth just didn't have much laughter in her today. Cindi pulled her over to where she was sitting and handed her a plate of fudge. "I can't have this, honey. I'm a diabetic."

"No, not anymore. Didn't they tell you that?" They had, but she'd forgotten. "We're having a debate on the flavors here. By the way, this was made with faerie magic, so you might just get a little bit of that buzz from it. Here, try this one. It's called peony. I've never even heard of that flower until today. Go ahead, try it."

MaryBeth sat down and picked up the small piece. "Oh, my goodness. It's just like you'd think one would taste." She was handed the raspberry one with a bit of honey. "I have always loved the taste of raspberries. This is good too. The little bit of honey makes me think of summer."

MaryBeth ate what they handed her. It was all in small portions, very tiny little bites that would be just enough for her to answer their questions about whatever it was she was tasting. By the time she was finished with the treats, she realized what they'd done to her. Not sure what to say to them, she let it go. MaryBeth did feel a little better, having eaten something.

"I have to say how glad I am that you said something to that reporter. If you'd not, I certainly would have. He got off easy with you." MaryBeth asked Wynter, another aunt of Theo's, what she might have done to him. "He'd not be walking around well, that's for sure. I just couldn't believe he was asking you anything, much less about your grandsons, right then."

"I couldn't believe it either, to be honest with you. My heart was hurting enough as it was without that thing stuck up in my face." She looked at Pem when she laughed a little. "Linda told me that she wished she could have been that brave as we were headed from the gravesite. Is there any more information on the others that were hurt?"

"They're all going to be going home soon. A couple of the officers are going to need home care, and we've arranged that for them." Winnie shook her head. "Sometimes I wonder what the hell this world is coming to. I don't mean just those boys—something was wrong with the two of them—but people in general. I'm sure the autopsy they're doing will show something was wrong with them rather than something wrong with the way they were raised. Not that I agree with talking to children when they need a good ass beating, but that's just me. Kids are too free with the way they treat people if you ask me."

"I saw a lady in the store yesterday with her two little ones. The older boy was tearing into loaves of bread and tossing the slices all over the store. His mother just stood there, telling him he wasn't to act that way. That she was going to give him a time out when they got home." Carson huffed. "I'd have given him a good bop on his ass and then made him clean the mess up."

"No, you wouldn't have. Your children wouldn't have acted that way in the first place." Grace said none of their kids would have. "It's not that I'm against talking to your children about things they're doing wrong. I mean, teaching them the difference between right and wrong is the only way to make sure they grow into good adults. But there are times when talking is not enough."

"I've spanked Pem here once or twice. That was all it took. And afterwards, I cried more than she did." Pem took her hand into hers and kissed the back of it. "The first time was when she told me she hated her father. I've never condoned the way Patrick treated her, but no one should hate their parent. I've since changed my mind in that regard. It is difficult to love someone when they treat you like Patrick did Pem. Or, for that matter, the way he treated his father and I. He was a difficult child and grew into a more difficult adult. I want you all to know I never raised them to be like that."

"Of course, you didn't." Each of them had a cup of tea in front of them that MaryBeth didn't remember being given. Taking a sip of the wonderful smelling brew, she was shocked when it filled to the top again. She looked at Cindi. "I'll leave you that cup. Once you fill it with something warm, not only will it stay at the same temperature, but it will refill when you need another cup. I've been drinking that particular brew for decades, and I simply love it."

They spoke about this and that for the rest of the hour before everyone was to show up. MaryBeth was called away, having been she had a phone call. As soon as she picked up the old-fashioned phone, she knew that it was Austin. He was terribly upset and sobbing.

"She's gone." MaryBeth asked him what he'd said. "Caroline is gone. She left me. She's gone, Momma. Gone."

~*~

Theo moved into the hallway to give MaryBeth some privacy. He went to find Winnie to ask her for her help. He had a feeling that something more than just Caroline being gone was bothering Austin. Even from across the room, he could hear the anguish of the man, his pain.

"I can get you there. Why are you going? If she's left him, there is little that we can do to get her back. Grief is like that." He told Winnie what he thought was going on. "Oh. I never— Let me have a quick look."

When she disappeared then returned, he opened his mouth to ask her what was going on. The next second, less he'd bet, he was standing in a house that he didn't know. He knew where he was. Theo could hear Austin sobbing into the phone just up the stairs.

Whatever he had expected, it wasn't Austin sitting on the floor in a very feminine bathroom. The phone was pushed against his ear, and he was holding a large gray bath towel to his face. There in the tub next to him was Caroline. She'd cut her wrist and killed herself. She hadn't left him. Caroline had left him behind.

"What are you doing here?" He took the phone away from Austin and told MaryBeth that he was there. After assuring her that he'd call her later, he put the cell phone in his back pocket. "She's left me, Theo. My wife is dead, and she left me."

"I know. I'm sorry. Austin, let's get you up from here. I'll call the police." Austin said he wasn't ready for them to come yet. "I know. But you're not going to end your life too. Come on, buddy. Help me get you up."

After getting him into his bedroom, Theo called the police. Telling him as best he could where to come, he finally had to find something with their address on it before he could guide them to the correct home.

"Are you sure she's dead?" He told them he thought she'd been gone for a few hours. "Don't touch anything, Mr. Manning. Someone is on their way. We'll also have the ambulance there. Don't touch anything."

"I haven't. I don't know if Austin did or not. He called me to come here when he found her." The officer asked him if he thought he'd killed her. "No. I believe, from the way he's talking, that he'd not known she was going to kill herself. He's upset that she left him behind."

"I'll send someone out there. Mr. Manning, we've all been made aware of what happened while they were gone. People in town, they're coming out of the woodwork to accuse the kids of one thing or another. I heard from one of my deputies just yesterday that the missus had been accosted when she was out in her yard bringing in their luggage. Someone had painted on their car too, some very nasty words." Theo asked him if they'd had a cruiser in the area since that happened. "We tried, but she ran us off last night. We'd had trouble with the boys too, but the parents have been treated badly since they returned without them. I'll send out a crew, Mr. Manning. If you could stay with Austin, I'd appreciate that."

Theo helped Austin get up again, this time from the bed. He wasn't helping him at all. Austin kept telling him that Caroline had left him behind. When Theo had enough, he slapped the man hard on the face. That got the desired effect.

"Are you listening to me now?" He nodded. "Say it, Austin. Tell me that you're going to listen to me and that you're going to get up off that lazy ass of yours and cooperate. The police are on their way to ask you some questions. First, I'm going to get you into the shower. All right? You stink."

"Yes, all right. I don't remember how long we've been home since we left your place." He told him it had been four days. "I miss them, Theo. I do, then I don't. They're my children, and I'm not entirely sure how I feel about them being gone."

"Understandable. Come on now. You're going to get your ass in gear here and go down to the living room so you can talk to the police. No fucking around. I'm going to fix you something to eat. If you're trying to kill yourself when I return, I'm going to help you along. But my way will be much more painful." He stared at him. "You think I'm joking with you?"

"No. I, the people in your town, they told me you were a dragon. Are you?" Theo nodded as he turned the man in the direction of the stairs. "I don't know what I'm going to do with myself. I'm all alone now, aren't I?"

"You've never been alone, Austin. You have a mother

and a niece that love you. They might not particularly like you, but they do love you. Go on in there and have a seat." He watched as he went into the living room and took a seat on the couch. "I'm going to make you something lite to eat, and you're not going to give me any shit about it."

As he made a sandwich for the other man, Theo spoke to his aunt. Telling her what he'd seen in the bathroom, she asked him to hold on. Winnie was a good person to contact for matters such as this. She'd be able to tell him if Austin had had anything to do with her death. It was his mom who spoke to him next.

I've summoned Caroline to me. You might want to know she's upset that Austin didn't find her before she was dead. I guess this is some sort of game she plays when she wants him to do something for her. She's also not at all happy that she's not with her sons on this side. I'm not sure how that was supposed to work with Austin saving her since she'd not told him what her plan was. Anyway, she wants to tell Austin that he'd better be joining her on the other side. Don't do that. I've been here talking to MaryBeth about what Austin told her, and she wants him to be all right. Even Pem wants him to come back here to start again. He asked her what she thought about that. *I'm not sure. But then, I'm not the one that would have to be around him all the time. However, I do think it might well be good for him to be away from his wife — dead or alive. She's a shrew and a big reason that the boys were never disciplined the way they should have been.*

I've called the police. I'm going to tell them I was staying here for a few days to make sure they got everything squared away. Not staying here but in a hotel. Can you have someone fix that up for me? Also, that he'd called me when he found Caroline. I'm sure calling his mom might be frowned upon, what with his dead wife no more than a few feet away from him. Mom said she'd have someone do that for him now. *Mom, he's not bathed since he's been here. And it looks like if there was any staff here when they returned, they've all left now. I'm going to have a few faeries out here to clean up the house and make sure nothing else happens to it while we take care of Austin.*

Good idea. I'll send a few of them along to get in touch with those that are there. If you can talk to him, see what he has to say about a few things. Carson gave me a list of things she can take care of on this end. After getting the list from her, he told her what he could about some of them. *Suicide isn't really anything that I know a great deal about, but I have to tell you, son, I think that if I lost one of you guys, I'd be hard pressed not to try it myself. I don't know what I'd do if anything happened to one of you.*

I've been thinking along those lines too. Trying to put myself in his place. I really don't know what I'd do if something were to happen to any of you. Theo told his mom what he was doing here and to keep an eye on Pem. *I didn't think to even let her know I was leaving. I had a feeling that Austin was calling to tell his mom goodbye, so I had Winnie bring me here.*

She knows where you are. It might be good for Austin to have her there as well. I'll have Winnie pop her in there.

Before he could tell her what a great idea that was, Pem was standing next to the couch like she'd been drinking something from a glass. *I think she might be there now.*

She is. I don't think Winnie even told her what she was doing. I'll talk to her. Theo laughed when Pem spoke to her uncle. *I'd better go. Pem is having it out with her uncle. I don't think it's going to end well for him.*

While they were on the couch talking, he let the police in. He asked them if they wanted to see the body first and took them there. Theo told them what he and his wife were doing there, as well as why he'd come over here before calling the police. He'd just not been sure about what Austin had told him about Caroline being gone.

"We came here to make sure they were all right. I know they're not, but wanted to make sure the funerals were just the way they wanted. We were set to leave today. I think Caroline might have known that." It was a lie, all of it, but the police didn't seem to wonder at his reasons. "Is there anything I can help you with, gentlemen? I don't want to leave Austin alone with my wife for too long. As you can well imagine, he's not doing so well."

After answering their question about whether he thought Austin might kill himself too, to which Theo said he thought he might, he went to the kitchen. The faeries had arrived with his own and were ready to take care of the home.

"There are officers here now, so avoid the upper floors until they say it's okay to clean the room. The kitchen and the refrigerator are in need of some cleaning as well as some food brought in. I don't know how long we'll be here, but I'd like to make sure there are at least some sandwich fixings until we leave." They were all right with that, telling him they'd stay for as long as he was there. "Good. Thank you so much. If you could perhaps keep an eye on the place too so that no vandalism occurs, even after we're gone. I don't know what is going to happen to this place, but I'd like to make sure it's here whenever we decide."

"We'll keep the intruders out, Lord Manning." He told him he was Theo. "Yes, my lord, we're aware of which dragon you are. Your lovely wife is all anyone can speak about. We'll make sure things are done to perfection."

When he went back into the living room, one of the officers was sitting on the couch across from Pem and Austin. Austin was crying off and on, but not nearly as badly as he'd been when he arrived. Pem was holding his hand, and Theo was glad for it. The three of them, including MaryBeth, might come out of this a little closer.

Theo kept an eye on the faeries as they flittered from room to room. The place had been left unattended for a few days, and things were piled up. Dust mostly, but there was mail on the dining room table that had to be dealt with. He found a couple pieces of hate mail that he turned over to the police. Even after they left, he stayed where he was in the dining room, going over what needed to be taken care of. Austin and Pem joined him there a few minutes later.

"I hope you don't mind, but I'm making arrangements on these for you. Most of them are past due, but they're going to allow me to pay them when I return home." Austin thanked him for that. "We have to talk about this, Austin. Not just about Caroline, but you as well."

"Pem said that one of your aunts speaks to ghosts." He said that was right. "I'm not saying I believe you, but I was wondering if they've spoken to Caroline or the boys. I know they're all gone, and I'm here alone, but I'd like to make sure that— Well, I don't really know what I'm making sure of, but I guess I wanted to find out why she did this. Or why the boys did what they did."

Theo glanced at Pem, and she shook her head a little. "My aunt said that the boys have moved on. They didn't stick around on the side of death for very long." He cried a little, and Theo let him before he spoke again. "Has Caroline tried to kill herself before, Austin? The reason I ask is, she had hoped that you'd find her before she was gone. Is that something you've done before?"

"Yes. Several times." He looked out the back door as he continued. "Whenever she didn't get her way, she'd do something like this. But last night—or the night before, I can't remember—I decided to take a few sleeping pills. Killing myself wasn't in my head then, not like it is now, but I just needed the thoughts in my head to go away, just for a little while. I don't know how long I was out, but I found Caroline the way she was when I went to find her. I thought we'd go to the grave today and talk to them. I have no idea. There wasn't any way for us to actually speak to them, but...." Austin looked at him, his face so full of anguish that he ached for the man. "They killed those men and women for no other reason than they could. I know that now. When I think of all the things, all the money that we had to pay out when they'd be up to no good, I wonder why it never occurred to me to get them help."

"Because of Caroline." It wasn't a question from Pem, but Austin nodded as he cried again. "She would get her way with things by saying she would kill herself. You have any idea how sick that is, Uncle Austin?"

"I do now." He looked at her. "So many times, I wanted to talk to you about what she was doing. It didn't seem to me that you were acting anything like she did when she did these things. I mean, the doctor even told me she was acting out. I didn't believe him, of course. I just couldn't understand anyone using such a dangerous thing to get my attention. But she never went too far. Understand?"

"Yes. I have to tell you both something. Something that I've only just recently found out myself. I've been...I guess you could say that I've been watched over since I was a small child. Not by anyone that I ever saw, but by a faerie. She told me today that she's so happy I found Theo. That she'd been keeping me safe for him for decades. I had no idea." Theo was going to have to find the little creature and thank her. He wondered who had sent her to watch over Pem and decided it had to be his mom or dad. They would have been able to see enough of his future to know that his mate was out there but might not make it to see him. "I never understood how someone would keep finding me when I would try to kill myself. It never seemed to matter where I was or how I'd taken care that no one could find me; I was always found. I know the reason why now."

"I love you, Pem." Pem told him that she loved him as well and laid her head on his shoulder. Austin was still staring out the window, and he wondered what the man was thinking. Getting up, he told him what they were going to do. Austin didn't argue with him when he told him he was going to take a shower. Instead, he got up and followed. Theo was worried about him. And his family. He was going to have to talk to MaryBeth before he made any decision concerning her son. The other one too.

Patrick was already causing trouble, arguing with the men who were set to work on the hospital. He'd either straighten up, or he'd find himself buried under the new facility. Theo had had about enough of his shit too.

Chapter 6

Pem smiled at her grandma when she came into the kitchen. "You've gone viral, Grandma. Look. People are loving you because you dressed down that news reporter." Grandma eyed the video of her and the reporter. "The Internet and the people on television are saying that you're the greatest thing that has ever hit the airways."

"I shouldn't have done that to that young man." Pem asked her why not. "He was only doing his job. I was angry in the first place, and you know it never ends well when you're upset and take it out on someone else. My goodness. What those people at the funeral must think of me taking away from what we were doing there."

"They interviewed Linda this morning." She backed the news station up until she found the point where they had spoken to Linda on the morning news. "Watch this, Grandma. You've made a difference in their lives. Not just Linda's, but a lot of people."

"...Yes. Tonight, we're going to have a meeting, the

families of the fallen and decide what to do with the things that have been donated. One television station donated fifty hams and turkeys for us to give away to others in need." The news reporter asked if they were going to give everything away. "That's what we're deciding on this evening. It's lovely. All of this for us to help others when we've had so many generous people giving when they could. Even being able to go to the grocery store for a few things is much nicer since there isn't a group of men and women on our lawn all the time shoving microphones and phones in our faces. I'm so happy that they're giving all of this the time to...well, for us to get used to being without our life partners. To grieve. I have thought of being without my husband. He was an officer, but the reality is so much worse than you think it will be. We have Mrs. Black to thank for us having the time to do what we so sorely need right now. Even though I know her heart is heavy too, she came to mine and the others' aid when we needed it most."

"Do you think she did that to appease her own feelings?" Pem watched her grandma as Linda stiffened up. Grandma did the same thing. "It was her grandchildren that—"

"Yes, it was. We all know that. Even if we didn't want to remember, you people would be reminding us all the time. She was at my house that morning, getting me up and out of bed. Making breakfast for the other children when my sister-in-law just didn't want to move. After arranging a sitter for me, she gently bullied me into getting a shower, getting dressed. Not one camera was there when she sat and cried with me. Telling me that she was so very sorry that it had happened to me. I didn't want to go to the service, because we'd be seeing my husband for the last time. It would be real then. His death like the others. But she didn't let me wallow in self-pity. MaryBeth told me that a lot of the people would be watching me and the others, and we had to make our husbands proud of us." Linda stood up then. "MaryBeth taught me something that day too. That when I don't care for something that is being said to me or about me, I don't need to let it go because I'm hurting. I need to stand up for myself and the others that might not be able to and make it right. Making it right is tossing you out of my house. Right now. That woman did this not because she had to, but because she wanted to. And I'm wanting you to get out of my home right now."

The news station was stunned. Everyone there at the place just looked at one another. But there was more, and Pem left it running even after they broke away for a commercial. Moving through the bit where they were advertising that there was a recall on lettuce, Pem stopped when the young news reporter was standing on the sidewalk outside of what she knew to be Linda's home.

"I must apologize to Linda. I was wrong in asking about the grandchildren of the Blacks. I was wrong, too, in what I said about Mrs. Black. I've never met the woman, but I have heard from other spouses of the officers that she'd been to their homes as well. Helping where she could, and even watching four little ones while the husband took a shower and had a few moments to himself. I am deeply ashamed of myself for what I did just now." She looked down the street, then back at the camera. "I wasn't threatened with termination for saying these things just now. Nor was I told that I'd better make it right. I'm saying this because I heartfully feel this way. I was no different than my counterpart at the funeral services, and I am deeply sorry for my actions."

Pem turned the television off and continued to watch her grandma. When she finally turned to her, Pem smiled. Her grandma had been through so much of late that it was really good to see her smile at things again.

"I spoke with Austin last night. He's going to come here for a little while. I don't know that living here is a good option, but he said that you and Theo had arranged it for him." Pem said that Theo had spoken to her last night too. "He was going to kill himself. When he called me here the other day, he told me that he was going to end his life to be with Caroline. He also told me that she'd done this sort of thing several times before."

"That's what Theo told me. Caroline was really pissed off that Austin didn't save her this time. Cindi, as you know, can see ghosts, and her thoughts on this thing with Caroline are that she deserved what she got. For crying wolf all the time when there wasn't anything there." Grandma nodded but didn't speak. "Uncle Austin wants to try and make amends for all the things he's done to not just you, but to everyone. Theo thinks he's sincere in what he wants to do."

"What do we do about Patrick?" Pem asked her how much she'd heard about him. "He's called here a few times. Twice while you were with Austin and Theo. He told me that since you were gone, I could have him stay here for a couple of nights without you knowing. I didn't let him just so you know."

"I know that, Grandma. You, of all people, would know what he's like more than anyone else. What did he want from you?" She told her. "Money. It's always about money with him, isn't it? I'm assuming he's asking you for it because he figures that since you sold the land, you might owe it to him or something?"

"Yes. That's just what he said. That since I'd sold off his inheritance, I should be forking over money to him when he wants it. When I mentioned that I might need it for my golden years, he told me he could help me along with that, so I could just give him all of it right now. I do believe he meant he'd kill me for it." Grandma looked at her again when she said that was what he was saying. "Do you really think he'd try and help me along toward my death so he could have money?"

"Yes." She hadn't even hesitated when she answered her. "When I was little, he would take Mom's pain medication so he could get high off it. I believe he even sold off a good deal of it as well. I'd put nothing past him. I keep thinking about him laughing when he was being taken back to his cell at the police station. Why?

What did he find that was so funny then?"

"I did the same thing, wondering about that. So, while I had him on the phone, I asked him. He said that the perfect Austin had children that were just like their good old uncle. That 'Mr. and Mrs. Perfect, my shit don't stink' had bad boys." Grandma got up to get down her teacup and put her finger on the rim. The hot brew filled the cup immediately. "I never thought I'd love this thing so much. To be able to have just a nice relaxing cup of tea makes me feel good."

Pem wondered if there was magic in the cup in addition to the magic to fill it. Something that would make sure that Grandma was less stressed. She decided she didn't care. So long as her grandma was enjoying it, it could have brandy in it for all she cared.

As Grandma sipped her brew, Pem got up to find some scones. These were something she never thought she'd enjoy as much as she did. Scones were the most wonderful invention ever as far as she was concerned.

They ate in silence for a few minutes. Grandma would sip her tea quietly. Pem was conscious of the sounds she was making chewing her treat. Just then, when someone knocked at the back door, both of them jumped in their seats and giggled. Pem got up to see who it was.

She'd been told she could see beyond the door. A few days ago, Theo had told her to be careful when she opened the door with her dad around. Putting her hand on the door, she could feel the person on the other side. It was her dad. Whatever he wanted, he was really pissed off about it. Moving back from the locked-up door, she touched her finger to her mouth to have Grandma not speak, and they made their way to the middle of the house.

"I don't want to have to deal with him, do you?" Grandma said she'd had enough of dealing with people for a lifetime. "Yes, I know what you mean. It's mostly just him. Always with his hand out, wanting me to give him something. He was like that with his dad too. If it wasn't money, it was something that would cost money."

The two of them stood in the pantry, a large open space between the dining room and the kitchen. Pem, to keep herself from going out there and braining her father, started opening cabinets to see what they had in them. She didn't remember ever being in this part of the house much more than to pass through.

"What the hell is this thing?" Grandma told her, and Pem laughed quietly. "What would I have a use for a cake breaker for?"

"My mother had one. I think there was one in the house Harold and I had as well. You cut cakes, like angel food cakes, with it. It's for a delicate cake you might bake. What did you think it was for?" Pem laughed, feeling her face heat up. "Now, I have to know."

"I thought it was some sort of comb you'd have to use when your hair was simply out of control. You have to admit, Grandma, that's what it looks like." She did agree with her, and Pem realized that she could no longer hear her father at the back door. "I was thinking that you and

I should take a little trip into town. I have a few things I'd like to pick up, and also some things to mail."

Theo had sent all the bills he'd been able to collect in her uncle's office back with her. There were quite a few of them too. It seemed to her that he was more past due on one bill than she had been in all her monthly bills when she'd been living alone. They'd not told anyone that they were helping him with his bills. She didn't care how anyone felt, but if Austin was to move back here, she didn't want anyone to look at him oddly. If it was his desire to start fresh, she wasn't going to have him worry about being able to make ends meet.

As they were coming down the stairs, she heard her dad out at the front door yelling. She heard him telling her to get her ass out there and to give him some money. She tore open the door just as he was taking in a deep breath to no doubt yell at her again.

"What the fuck do you want?" He drew back his fist as to hit her, she thought. "You do, and they'll never fucking find where you stood last. Tell me what you want so I can tell you no and go on about my business."

"I want you to give me some money. Not a pittance either. I want some real money." She said as far as she knew, all money was real money. "Don't be a bitch, Pem. Give me some right now. I'm your father, and you should be giving me some of what you have in the first place. Living here in this big house, you should be able to at least hand over a few things I can pawn. That should keep me until you get some cash on you."

"Why is it you're only my father when you want something from me? Not that it matters—you've never been a real father to me anyway. I'm not going to give you money. Nor am I going to give you a place to live. You're not welcome here any more than you were when I lived at my other place. Go away." She felt her grandma come up behind her. Dad looked at her and opened his mouth. "Grandma isn't going to give you anything either. We're finished with your shit."

"Mom, I'm in a hard place here. I haven't got anywhere to live. I don't have anything for food. Even the places I've been thinking on staying are gone. And that's all your fault. How could you tear down our family home? I had plans of living there until such time as you could afford to get me a place of my own. You know, you should want to give me money. My kid didn't embarrass you like Austin's did. I always knew those kids of his were mean. I mean—"

"Do shut up, Patrick. I've a headache, and it's your fault. I didn't tear the house down. The construction company did. But it mattered little to me that they did it as I no longer owned the land. I made a nice tidy profit, and I'm thrilled to be living here with Pem and her lovely husband, Theo." Grandma came around her and poked Pem's father in the chest with her finger as she continued. "Those boys didn't embarrass me. You are the one that does that, every day you're upright. Get a job, Patrick. You're much too old for me to have to support you. Not that I ever did once you started whaling on Pem. When

Austin arrives, I expect you to stay away from him as well."

"Austin and Caroline are going to move in there with you guys? That's fucking wrong. What the hell did he do that makes him so special? Nothing, I tell you. Nothing at all but to raise up two of the worst kids in the history of all kids being born." Grandma told him he was the close second. "You're just being mean now. There isn't any call for you treating me like this, Mom. I'm the good one. If they get to live there, then I'm going to—"

"Caroline is dead." Pem could tell that he'd not known that. Only telling him the highlights, Pem continued with what she thought he needed to know. "She killed herself several days ago. Austin was ready to join her, but Theo was there to help him get his shit together. And he did. Unlike you, he's going to get himself a job here and support himself."

Dad started laughing, like hearing about his brother and his burdens were the funniest thing he'd ever heard. As soon as she had enough, Pem moved by him to her car. Her father had a way about him that no matter how hard she tried to stand up to him, he would end up making her cry. Grandma joined her a few minutes later and simply got in and buckled her seatbelt.

"I've told the staff that he was around, so they'd know to kick his ass if he tried anything." Pem thanked her grandma. "No need for that. I've been thinking about Austin since this incident with your father. I want him to come here and try to get his shit together. Just like you said. If he doesn't…. Well, with this family, we have ways of scaring people straight. Perhaps I should think of a way to get Theo to burn Patrick a little. Might do him a bit of good to know that this family isn't one to mess with. What do you think?"

"I think you're brilliant. And I love you." She kissed her grandma on her cheek and looked out her front window to see her dad being chased off by a pack of wolves. "That's a wonderful sight. Don't you think?"

"I hope they bite him in the butt."

They were both still laughing when they got into town. There were a few places they could shop, but decided to get lunch first. She loved spending time with her grandma, and she decided she was going to do it more often. Pem only hoped Austin would get his shit together as he claimed he wanted to do. If he didn't, Pem thought Grandma had the best idea. She'd have Theo or one of the others take care of him.

~*~

Theo couldn't wait to get home. He did feel pretty good about getting some things done for the other man. His bills were paid off, his house was on the market, and he had been able to get Caroline buried by her sons. The red tape concerning that had had him calling his Aunt Carson. There were only two spots, and the boys had taken up both spaces. Getting one more casket in the same plot had been taken care of by her.

Austin had decided to live near his mom to get to know her better. He had also decided to sell off his house.

Theo had been concerned for a while that the state was going to take it from him. The families of the dead that had been killed by his sons were willing to forego the money he might have coming to him by way of selling his home. They were going to take the insurance money that had been in Caroline's name. It had been worth a great deal more than the house would have been anyway. It might not sell either, and that was the biggest factor in them taking the insurance money. Aunt Carson had rushed it through. The fact that it hadn't had a suicide clause in it was all that had saved Austin.

The contents of the house were being donated to the shelter house nearby. Anything of value, they'd packed up and taken with them. There was a pitiful amount of that too. As they were seated on his family's plane, Theo asked Austin if he was all right.

"I don't rightly know how to answer that, to be honest with you. You've done more for me than I believe I ever did for my own flesh and blood in all these years." Theo told him they were family. "I'm sure you're just saying that because you have to. But whatever the reasons behind it are, I'm grateful for your help. Once the house is sold, if it ever does, I won't have a single reason to go back home. If you're thinking I'm a terrible man for not wanting to visit the graves of my family, I do have a reason for it."

"You can tell me if you wish. But I don't think you're being terrible. As you told me the other day, you need to make your own way in this world. Coming back there to visit the graves of your family won't be moving forward, but only back." He nodded. "You're going to be just fine, Austin. I know it. You've got a good head on your shoulders, and you are making sound decisions."

"I should be in prison." He'd said this to him before since he'd been at his home with him. "I know you keep telling me that I had no way of knowing anything like that was going to happen. But I also know I didn't pay as much attention to the boys as I probably should have. Or at the very least, kept up with what the neighbors and the schools were telling me."

"Yes, you should have. But beating yourself up over it now, at this late date, isn't going to bring them back. Nor will it bring Caroline back. As you said, Caroline was a grown woman playing deadly games. It was bound to happen, one of the times she played with her own livelihood, that you'd not be there in time to make sure she was treated. I told Pem that you were going to be volunteering with the suicide hotline. She does as well three nights a week." Austin told him he might learn a thing or two himself. "I don't doubt that one bit. Even Pem said she was dealing with her depression a lot less than she had been since she's been working the phones."

Pem was waiting at the end of the ramp for them. MaryBeth was there as well, but he only wanted his mate. Grabbing her up when she leapt into his arms, she kissed him all over his face until she'd had enough. Looking over at her uncle, she grinned at him then told him that she'd missed Theo.

"I can see that." They all looked toward where MaryBeth was still standing. "Is she upset that I'm here?"

"No. She's not sure how she feels about you living here, but she is willing to meet you halfway. I think you should understand that she's also afraid you'll get into her heart again then leave. I don't know that she can take that a second time, Uncle Austin." He told Pem that he wanted this to work as well. "Then I suggest you take the first step toward that and go hug your mom. She needs it too."

Theo set Pem down on the floor, and they walked hand in hand toward Austin and his mom. They were talking quietly, which Theo thought was the best way for the two of them to start off. As soon as Austin wrapped his arms around his mom and started crying, he hoped it was good news.

"Mom and I are going to work on this. I can't tell you how happy I am about that." Pem told him it was showing. "I hope so. We have a lot of years to make up for. A great many more hurts, but I'm going to do everything I can so that Mom and I can be together."

"Good." Grandma hugged Pem, then him. "I'm so glad you helped him out, Theo. You're a good man and a better grandson-in-law than a woman could ask for."

"I'm hoping to get lucky later." MaryBeth smacked him on his chest as she moved toward the outdoors to the little airport. "I've had some people meet the plane at the tarmac, and they're going to bring the things that we brought back with us to the warehouse. Austin is going to be staying with us until the sale of his house. Then he's going to be looking for a place of his own unless he finds himself an apartment. He's going to be looking for a job as well."

"I've not had a job in a long time. I mean, other than just calling in my orders for the day at the business I was supposed to be running. I'm actually kind of looking forward to it. I'd like a job where I can be around people." Pem was telling him about the waitstaff job that was opening up in the local pizza shop. "Really? I might apply for that. I really do want to work around the public. It might not be such a good idea right now, not with everyone still hurting from what happened, but I'm willing to do it."

"I can talk to the owner for you. I know her from some of the meetings I'm working on for the new hospital and the staffing there. When we begin to hire there, we're going to be hiring several hundred people before it's up and running completely."

Theo was glad that Pem had gotten some advice from his mom when she'd been there for the funeral. She'd told Pem that there was all kinds of work that needed to be done behind the scenes. Mom had even given her a list of things that she could startup with the help of Rachel. Not busy work, but things that would help the community as a whole.

It's what he and his brothers had been doing since they got there, working small to work up to the larger things that the town and its people needed. Even when he'd not been home for the last few days, Theo had managed to set up someone to go to all the empty building just off the main street and see which ones could be used after a thorough clean up, as opposed to which would need a huge overhaul.

Milo was working on getting some garden spaces cleaned up and ready for spring. There would be access to water, as well as a tractor to use for a small price. Hadley had someone helping him with getting some people in town to start up a new business, as Finn and Dover were working with Pem to get the hospital staff in place. The building was going up well, and there were things they could get going now, even before they had their first patient.

"I'd like to take you all to dinner." Theo told MaryBeth she didn't need to do that. "Of course, I don't need to do it. I'm doing it because I want to. It will be nice. And I'm certainly in a position of being able to afford it."

Getting into the limo, Theo kept an eye on Austin. He was doing well, he thought. His face wasn't as tense and pinched looking as it had been. When Pem nudged him, she put out her hand, and a small little man was there. MaryBeth had gotten her faerie just a few days ago. She and Mildred seemed to be getting along just fine.

"Austin, this is Becker." Austin stared at the tiny little man Theo had pointed to and nodded. "He's not a faerie, but a brownie. He would like to stay with you, all the time. He'll keep you company when you need it and can be quite helpful when you need that as well. If for some reason, the two of you don't work out, Becker will be fine with that. He's a little bit to get used to."

"He only says that because it's true." Becker laughed and flew to Austin when he put his hand out. "Oh, but you're hurting, aren't you, Mr. Austin? My goodness, you need to smell the flowers. There is nothing in this world that smelling a few dozen flowers won't heal."

"I have been hurting, but I'm feeling better." Becker told him, of course, he would be. "Why are you hard to get along with, Becker? If you don't mind me asking."

"I don't mind nary a bit. I am hard on a body because I'm just me. I have a good time and expect you to have one too. Also, I tend to tell the stupidest jokes. I think they're funny when I hear them, but then I mess them up something terrible when I tell them. I get around to it eventually, but by then, I've lost my audience." Becker laughed once again. "Also, when I get it about right, I tend to get too excited to finish it, and that can be aggravating as well. I do try."

"I'm not good at jokes at all. It's been pointed out to me that I have no sense of humor." Becket looked very upset about that. "Perhaps you can teach me a few. That way, we can be the best slapstick duo ever born."

Becket turned to him. "I like him, Lord Theo. I think the two of us are going to be getting on just fine. Just fine indeed." Austin laughed. It was the first time since he'd met the man that he'd heard it. Austin seemed as surprised by the noise as everyone else did.

By the time they pulled up in front of the restaurant,

Theo realized how hungry he was. Glad that they were shown a table right away, he started in on the breadsticks that came with the meal. If this kept up, he was going to have to start eating a meal before he left to go get one. He didn't want to make MaryBeth broke on their first outing as a family.

Theo liked the sound of that. Family. They were his too. Even though they'd gotten off to a bad start, they were coming together now. They just needed to take care of a couple of things, Patrick being one of them, and they'd be all right. He did remember Sandra then, but she was going to prison, despite what she told anyone that would come around. Merkle's Mark was going to be opening soon, and he was looking forward to that. Even his parents were coming back to enjoy the grand reopening. Things were, he thought, moving right along.

Theo knew they were far from out of the woods with the things that had happened. There were still people in the hospital. The police department needed to be filled out again. Theo missed his good friend Amos, but he knew that when it was a good time to hire a new chief, the town would do a great job of that as well.

Chapter 7

Patrick had had enough of going around without any money. It wasn't like his mom didn't have any to hand to him. Even his own daughter was living it up in a nice fancy house and acting like there wasn't a thing in the world for her to worry about. What about him? He should have been on top of her list of shit to worry about. Not that man she had married. He was a dork anyways, if you asked him. Who the hell did he think he was acting like his wife's dad didn't matter squat?

Then there was Austin. It really got in his craw that Austin was being welcomed into Pem's house. By rights, it should have been Patrick's house too. Living with them in the fancy house should have been something he was doing. Even his own mom wouldn't allow him to stay a couple of nights by sneaking him into the house. No one should be treated this way when there was money to be had.

He saw Austin as he walked to the pizza place. It would be just like him to go in there and have himself a good meal. Patrick hadn't had himself a good meal since—well, he couldn't remember. About the time that his missus took sick. She sure could make a pork chop be glad that it was in her skillet, that's for sure.

There hadn't been any insurance on his wife. When he'd gone to the insurance company he'd had his car insurance with, he asked them when he was going to get his wife's pay off. The man stared at him for several long seconds as if he didn't understand.

"You know. A death benefit. Where is my wife's? I would have thought that since she'd been gone for a few months, you'd have hunted me down for it." He told him that it had only been two weeks. "Whatever the time, where is my money? Everybody knows that when someone dies, there is insurance to be had. I would like to get hers."

"She didn't have any insurance." Patrick had pointed out that everyone had insurance. "You think they just automatically give an insurance payout when someone dies? Well, it doesn't work that way. You have to take a policy out, then make the payments on it every month. If your way were the way to go, then there wouldn't be any insurance companies around. No. Neither you nor your wife had any life insurance policy. I can help you set up one for you. The policy won't cost you that much per month. I can even—"

"Are you telling me that there isn't any money coming from her up and dying? I was sort of counting on that money. To, you know, have me some new things.

I mean, what are you even in business for if you don't provide people with a means to get some nice payout when someone dies?" He told him that he was in the business of selling insurance, not paying out for anyone that dies. "Well, that just sucks. Here I was thinking you all were going to give me a hefty payout when she died, and you're sticking it to me. I should call the police on you is what I should do."

"You go right ahead and do that, Mr. Black. And when they stop laughing, I'm sure they're going to tell you the same thing. That unless you paid for it, there won't be any payout." He explained to him the way it worked had Patrick paying for the insurance every month. It wasn't a payout so much as it was him getting all his money back at one time. That made no sense at all. "I think it's time you left. You might want to think about getting a policy for yourself too. I'm sure that lovely daughter of yours could use some help in paying for your funeral."

That had been when his wife had passed on. Patrick hadn't paid for his car insurance anymore, either. If they didn't payout on a big thing like death, then they'd surely find some reason not to pay him if he was to wreck his car. Some people didn't deserve to be in business, Patrick had thought then and now.

Standing on the spot where he thought his parents' home had been, he looked out over the area. He'd not known that they'd had so much land when he'd been living here. Had he figured it out, he would have surely had them sell it off to keep him in cash. Or he would have done it on his own. Damn it all to hell and back, they had cheated him. Austin too, but he had money when he married that bitch Caroline.

She'd turned her nose up at him every time he saw her like she was so much better than he was. Patrick had always told Austin that he'd married beneath himself by marrying Caroline, but Austin said she was a good woman and he loved her. Love?

"That right there is the ruination of the world. Love isn't good for anyone." He looked around when he realized he'd been speaking aloud. People tended to look at you sideways when they heard you doing that.

Patrick decided to see if he could get himself some money by stealing one of the big rigs that was working on the land thereabouts. They were a mite bigger than he'd thought they were. Standing right up close to one of them, he realized that the wheels on the suckers were larger than he was. He could have made him a whole house by living in one of them too, he thought with a laugh. Walking around the big yellow monster, he couldn't for the life of him figure out how someone was supposed to get into the thing.

"Can I help you?" He turned and looked at the man standing there. Big man too, dressed in a nice suit that fit him like it was made just for him. Patrick tried holding in his belly but couldn't breathe and talk while doing that. "Is there something I can help you with, Mr. Black? I would like to point out that you're on private property. The fence you knocked over had a sign hung on it that states that. In the event you missed it while breaking and entering."

"I was going to have me a little fun with this thing. How do you suppose them guys get into this sucker?" The man told him he wouldn't know but that he should move along. "You're not very friendly, are you? Well, I want you to know that my daughter's family owns this here land, and she said I could come here and have myself a little fun. No harm in having some fun, now is there?"

"It is when you trespass and try to steal a piece of equipment that doesn't belong to you." He said that his daughter said he could have a time on it. "I'm your daughter's brother-in-law, and I know for a fact that she'd not let you touch any of this equipment, much less tell you to have some fun with it."

"What the hell? Is she fucking related to everyone in town? Which one are you?" He told him his name. "What kind of name is Milo? Sounds fake if you ask me. Anyway, you call her up and ask her about it. While you're doing that, I'm going to figure this thing out and have me a couple of turns with it."

"What are you doing here, Dad?" He turned too quickly and fell over. Neither his daughter nor the two men with her offered to help him up. "Hello, Milo, thanks for calling us. As you know, I wouldn't allow him on the property to take a pee, much less a large piece of equipment to take a joy ride in. His plan more than likely was to steal it."

"Give me some money, Pem, and I'll pretend that this never happened." She told him no and that nothing had happened. "Damn it, girl. What the hell is wrong with you anymore? You used to be good enough to tap for some cash when you was younger. I might have to resort to that sort of tapping again if you don't pay up."

The low growl from both the men scared Patrick enough that he backed away from Pem. Neither one of them moved, nor did they take their eyes off him. Patrick felt his asshole tighten up like it knew before his brain did that something was about to get jiggy here.

"I wasn't gonna hurt her. You're too close." That got him another growl, this one from the man he knew to be her husband. "You got no cause to be scaring me like that. I've done nothing wrong to any of you. I just need me some flashing around money until I can get me a big payoff from my mom. She said she'd help me out."

"No, she didn't. And while I haven't any idea what flashing around money is, you're not going to get anything from me. Nor grandma. Why don't you get yourself a job? Uncle Austin did. He's working at the pizza shop, and he's excited to start working soon." Patrick looked at where he'd seen his brother go. "Dad, you're a grown man and shouldn't be depending on anyone for you to have housing and food. Get your shit together and get your life on track. Otherwise, you're going to be found in an abandoned house frozen to death come winter."

"Winter is a few months away. I got plenty of time to get myself some money." He put out his hand. "Why don't you be the first to donate to me finding me a house like you have and a nice cozy income too?"

They turned and walked away. Just before they were through the fence where there was a lock and chain, Theo, he thought his name was, turned back. He had a big shit-eating grin on his face, a term his dad had said a lot. Patrick had never understood that, either. Who would want to eat shit?

"It doesn't mean that at all, moron. Shit eating grin means that I'm giving you a self-satisfied smile. As in, I know something you don't. Which really isn't saying much. I think the dirt you're standing on is smarter than you are." Patrick looked down at the dirt, then at the bottoms of his shoes. He didn't get that either. Then he realized the man knew what he was thinking. "Of course, I know what you're thinking. It's not hard. You're too stupid to be aware that it's happening all the time. Get off this land, Patrick, or the wolf pack that scared you from our home will bite you hard this time."

He heard the howling just before they showed up at the other end of the land he was standing on. They were surely eating up the distance to get to him. Rushing to the opening that the others were at, he was pissed when they shut the gate before he got there and put the lock on. Christ almighty, he was going to be eaten alive.

He didn't know how he'd made it, but he got out of the broken fence with only a few bite marks. Patrick tried to look at the marks they'd made on his backside. His ass was bloodied, but he still had it. Walking toward a place he'd been staying, the homeless shelter, he was about ready for something to go his way.

"Mr. Black, you're dripping blood on the floor. You're going to have to go get that taken care of before I allow you inside." He told the lady at the front desk at the shelter that he was going to see the nurse. "She's here only on Fridays. Today is Wednesday. You'll have to go get it taken care of at the clinic or not stay here. We have strict policies on bloodborne pathogens."

"On what?" She opened her mouth, and he decided he couldn't stand to hear her using that voice of hers again. "Why don't you have signs that tell people this shit? I mean, it would be nice to know it before I get here."

"Watch your language. I will not tell you again. There are signs all over the place once you get inside the door. Perhaps you should take the time to read them." Patrick tried to get on her good side, telling her he'd not thought to look at them when he was greeted with such a lovely face right when he came in. "Be that as it may, you're to get yourself fixed up before you can return. Have a nice evening."

He often wondered if people realized that saying have a nice whatever wasn't really going to happen. It was like they were giving you one more stick of a knife before they slammed the door in your face. Patrick had had enough doors slammed in his face for several lifetimes. The fuckers. When was he going to get his due? Never, it seemed. Not even a little bit of cash from his fucking family.

The clinic was packed. There were snotty brats all over the place. One of them was eyeing him like he was some kind of tasty meal. A couple of them came to talk to him, asking him if he'd read them a story.

"No. Go away, kid. I don't have time for your shit today. Can't you see I'm hurting?" The kids went back to their moms, and he got the stink eye from them. He thought people were way too sensitive nowadays. All they wanted to do was blame everyone else for their lot in life.

Patrick had always known he was lazy. In fact, he embraced the idea of being the laziest slob ever created. Why should a person work for a living when there were so many ways to not have to work? Like when his missus would go down to the mall at Christmas and put Pem's name on one of those little soldiers or whatever that hung on the tree. People would take the name, buy whatever was on the list, and then send it to the house.

Putting his own name on one of the cards had worked for a few years. He'd gotten some really fun stuff. Then some old bitty had noticed his name, and he'd been barred from getting anything. Even his kid had been taken off the list. His wife had been powerful mad at him for getting Pem knocked off the list too.

When he was finally called to see the doctor, the doctor took one look at the bite marks and told him he couldn't do anything. That they'd been made by a wolf. Patrick asked him what that had to do with anything.

"Well, you were bitten by an alpha, a wolf in charge of

his pack. The only way these will stop bleeding and seal up is for the alpha to forgive you for your transgressions. Meaning you have to tell him you're sorry for doing whatever he caught you at to have bitten you. You have to mean it too." Patrick told him that was the stupidest thing he'd ever heard. "That's the way it works. I'm sorry."

"Are you sorry enough that you can just slap something on them so that I can get into the shelter tonight? Miss Picky Butt said that with me bleeding, I can't stay there. Something about a path being made up or something." He told him that it would continue to bleed. "So? I just need to get someplace to sleep tonight, and I'll find the alpha tomorrow. It's been a stressful day for me."

After having his ass numbed up, the nurse cleaned the wound up for him. Using her phone, she took a picture of his ass cheeks and showed it to him. Damn, but they'd gotten him good. Leaving the clinic, he was feeling pretty good. One thing in his life had gone according to plan.

As soon as he was in front of the shelter, he knew he was going to be finding himself someplace else to sleep tonight. The fucking place closed the doors at seven. According to the clock on the town square that had been there since he'd been a kid, it was five after.

"Mother fuck."

He pounded on the door, knowing someone had to be in there. But no one came out to let him in. Patrick was going to have to have a word with someone about this shit, just as soon as he could figure out who. Damn it all to fuck and back. He didn't want to sleep outdoors.

Poor Patrick. You're having a shitty night, aren't you? He looked around to find the person making fun of him. *When I bit you earlier tonight, I got a bit of your blood. Now I can talk to you anytime I want. You should know better than to try and steal from the Mannings. They've given me permission to do whatever I want to you. Isn't that just great? I decided I'm going to play with you a bit before I have to crush you. And trust me when I tell you, I plan on making your last days on this earth a very difficult time for you.*

"You need to come and fix my ass. It's hurting again now that that shit has worn off." The man just laughed. "There isn't a damned thing funny about biting a man in the butt area. Didn't your momma teach you not to bite?"

No. She was a very big supporter of biting whoever I wanted when they screwed around with me. Now that I'm alpha, I can tell you that biting someone that needs it gives me all kinds of perks. Like with you sharing your blood with me, I'm able to make you dance like a puppet. Patrick actually felt his legs tingle with the need to do just what he'd said to him. *Dance, Patrick.*

Patrick was still dancing around like a damned fool several hours later. The police had run him in too. While he'd been trying to make his legs and arms stop moving, he'd broken the front glass out of the store. They were telling him it was breaking and entering. No matter how many times he told them he'd not entered, they still ran him in. During the rest of the night, he danced to a tune that he didn't hear. Christ, he was going to murder him, someone. And soon too.

~*~

"I tell you, it was the funniest thing I'd ever seen in all my life. And I've seen some pretty funny shit too." George could hardly contain himself as he was telling the story of seeing Patrick dancing down the sidewalk. Theo was laughing with him because he was having such a good time telling the story. "He must not have a bit of tone in his head because whatever he was dancing to, it looked like he didn't get the beat down. Christ, it was all I could do to breathe while watching the moron."

"Peter called here and told me what he'd done. I would have gone out to see him too, but I was stuck here with my lovely wife." Pem smiled at him. "I'm glad he's safely behind bars now. If he keeps pissing people off, we won't have to worry about him getting into the house. Someone will murder him for being stupid."

Finn and Rachel were coming over for dinner tonight. George had stopped by the house to tell them what he'd found out about Patrick, and he was staying too. The others all had things they were taking care of but said they'd be by later for dessert. There had better be some leftovers, too, Dover had told him.

Rachel came back into the living room after she'd been called away for a phone call. "That was the doctor's office that was to look at Sandra. He said she's fit to stand trial. He did recommend to her that she shouldn't be her own attorney, but that has nothing to do with him.

Doctor Bing gave her a clean bill of health and sent her back to jail." Theo explained some of what was going on with Sandra to Pem the other day, so she was up to speed. Austin asked how she was related to them. "My sister-in-law. Or she was. She was married to my brother for a little while. They've since divorced, but because she didn't say he could leave her, then they're still married as far as she's concerned—whatever. She's off her noodle. When we reopen Merkle's Mark, I think we should have one of the officers let it slip. Just to see what she has to say about it."

They were all still laughing at their families when they were called to dinner. The doorbell rang just as Theo was walking by it, and he told Samson, their new butler, that he'd get it. There was a woman standing at the door looking at the driveway when Theo asked her if she needed help.

"I'm here to find Doctor Black. She's Army. I was told she lives here with someone by the name of Manning." He said that was him. "Is Doctor Black here? I mean, this is what I was told, but some people think it's really funny to send people on a wild goose chase. Did you know you have wolves on your land?"

"I do. They're the local pack. You must not have ill intent in your heart, or you would never have gotten by them. Do you know Doctor Black?" She said they'd served together in the service. "All right. Come on in, and I'll get her for you."

"Thanks. Do you suppose I could have a glass of

water and a couple of aspirin? I have a fucking killer of a headache." He stood at the doorway to the dining room and told Pem she had a visitor. He could have gotten her a glass of water and whatever else she needed, but he didn't move. As soon as Pem came around the doorway to the dining room, the other woman's face lit up like a Christmas tree. "I knew you'd be in some cushy house with your feet propped up. How the hell have you been?"

The two women hugged, and he made his way to the kitchen to ask for another plate to be put at the table. While he waited, he grabbed some aspirin and a small glass of water for the stranger. When he returned to the dining room, Pem was telling everyone who the woman was.

"This is Doctor Jamie Darkhouse. She was my go-to anesthesiologist when we worked together overseas. She's really good at her job too." Jamie shook hands with everyone at the table and sat down next to Pem when George moved down a seat. "The last time I saw you, you were having some trouble with Pecker Head."

"Yes. He got his comeuppance right before I came home. I'm here to see to some things, then head back to my place to live out the rest of my days, I guess. I'm not going to be able to re-up, but that's neither here nor there." Theo watched the two of them and could tell that they were very good together. They didn't go as far as finishing sentences, but he could tell they would work very tightly together. Jamie was telling them about the last few days that Pem was on duty. "She'd been shot up to fuck and back. The idiot that operated on her said that he was going to leave one of the bullets in her to keep her from taking his job. He should have known I'd say something to someone. Anyway, he was discharged a few days after Pem here got her walking papers. By the way, I heard what Doctor Shivas did to you. A lot of women are singing your praises right about now."

"He made a pass at me, an unwanted one, and then told me he could get me some drugs to help with the depression. He also told me that depression wasn't real and that I was only doing it for show. I dislocated his arm when he touched me and sent him to the floor." Jamie laughed and said how they'd had to put it back in its place, and she'd been there. "I bet he milked that for all he was worth too."

"You know it." Jamie looked around the table. "Christ, you guys are huge. I'm sure you've heard that before. But damn, I'm also thinking that none of you are human. Maybe some more of the wolves running around?"

"Dragon." She nodded, and he watched her face. When she smiled at him, he had a feeling that whatever came out of her mouth now would be forever funny to them. "You don't have a problem with us being dragons, do you?"

"No. But I was thinking about the old saying about a bear shitting in the woods. I'm guessing when you guys do, you leave quite a pile. I haven't any idea where that thought came from, but there you have it." She put out her hand, and before he took it, he told her that she might get a zap from him. "That's all right, Theo. I'm not long for this world anyway, so you go ahead and zap me all you want."

As soon as he put his hand around hers, he could feel it. Not only was she not long for this world, but it was happening sooner than even the doctors knew. He told her he was sorry. After waving him off, he asked her what she was doing hanging around there.

"My sister. She's been in a nursing home since she was hurt when my parents were. I turned over my share of her insurance so that she'd continue to have care. Two weeks ago, I was informed that her money was all gone and that I'd have to see about taking her on my own. I can't, so that is where I'm headed in the morning." He asked her if she had a place to stay. "I'm staying at my parents' home. Well, it's mine, but I'm going to be staying there."

"Holy shit. You're Jamie Darkhouse." She nodded at George. "Let me rephrase that. You're part of the Darkhouse family that lives right outside of town. In the large mansion there."

"Yes. Mansion it is, but worth nothing. It was in poor repair even before they were both killed. Now it's an eyesore. The town wants to buy it, but I just can't bring myself to let it go. I will soon enough, but it's just that I spent a great many holidays there growing up with my family. Not always good ones, mind you, but we had a few of them." Pem asked her what she meant by letting it go soon; she'd said something like that three times now. Jamie looked at him before she answered. "I have a rare blood disease attacking my body. While it's doing that, it's shutting down my major organs one at a time. The doctor said I have a few months left, but I bet if you asked Theo here, he'd have a better count. Don't you?"

"You have less than three weeks if that." She nodded and looked at Pem. "I can help you, Jamie. I'd be glad to help you out with this."

"Naw. I don't have much to go on for any more. I mean, my death will pay off my sister's bill and pay for me to be burned up, and that's it. I'm worth more to her dead than alive." Theo asked if her sister would think that. "She hasn't any idea who I am. Who anyone is, for that matter. She was in the same car accident that killed my parents. Massive head injury that caused her to be without oxygen for too long. She can get up and move around, but she doesn't talk, feed herself, or even know how to dress herself. Walking is about it. Only, they told me, because she was just learning that when she was hurt."

"I'm so sorry." He watched as Pem hugged the other woman. Touching his fingers to her back, he sent as much magic as he could to her without her knowledge. Pem kissed him on the mouth when they separated. "No matter, you'll stay here until we figure things out. I won't take no for an answer. Also, I want to look into the money with your sister. You told me about that once. How there was an investment firm to watch over her money. I'm going to get to the bottom of that too."

"She's always been like that. Never leaving any stone uncovered." Theo handed a bowl of mashed potatoes to Jamie to touch her. She was already getting better. "I lost my favorite pen once. Three weeks later, she brings it to me, telling me she finally chased it down. I didn't tell her then that I'd already bought one to replace it. She might well have hit me with it."

The rest of the main meal was like that. Laughter was all over the place. Theo also noticed that Finn made it a point to touch the young woman too. Even George, who wasn't a dragon, gave her a little of what he had. Theo would bet in no time, Jamie was going to get a clean bill of health. Then perhaps she could help him talk Pem into being head of surgery at the new hospital. They'd make a hell of a team if they would work together. Finn nodded at his other brothers when the meal was being cleared away for dessert.

Chapter 8

Jamie watched Dover as he moved behind her. Then when he shook his head at Finn, she stood up. This shit was getting on her last nerve. He'd been the third brother to move behind her and sniff. The fuckers were treating her like a nasty dog.

Pushing the big man to the wall, she grabbed his, what turned out to be an impressive handful of balls and squeezed them tightly. The look of pain on his face was just what she was going for.

"What the fuck are you looking for?" He glanced at his brother, and she squeezed just a little more. Smiling at him, knowing that her eyes did not reflect her being in a good mood, she asked him again. "I'm talking to you, not him right now. Why are you fuckers going behind me and sniffing me like a mangy dog?"

"You'd be a bitch, not a dog." She gave his balls a hard yank. "Sorry. Sorry. Sorry. I was trying for humor. I don't think you're going to be in any better of a mood when I tell you what— All right. Yes. To the point. Finn told us to do it."

Finn was moving out of the room when she pulled a knife from her boot and threw it toward him. The sharp blade was still vibrating when she told him to stop. When she moved across the room, Finn turned to look at the knife then at her when she did the same to him. Only instead of using her hand to his manly parts, another knife had him standing still.

"Honey, she has a knife to my cock and balls."

Jamie didn't turn to see what Rachel might be doing. For all she knew, the women could have been holding a gun toward her. But right now, Jamie wanted answers.

"Rachel, honey, she's going to cut them off."

"I'm impressed that she understood that you were fucking with her livelihood. I told you, several times, not to do this. To be straightforward to her and to tell her. But oh no. Not Finn Manning. You had to be all stealthy, didn't you?" Jamie could hear the humor in Rachel's voice when she asked Pem for some more whipped cream on her pie. "The next time I tell you something, it might well help you to listen to me. Women aren't as dumb, nor as unobservant, as you and the rest of your brothers think we are."

"She's right, you know." Finn nodded. "You're an idiot if you think for one second you can pull shit like sniffing me like I'm some tasty stew, and think I'd not understand that you're feeling me out for a part of this family. You fucker, did you even think to wonder what one of your brothers would do if they were stuck with a mate that only had weeks to live?"

"You don't. I mean, you might well have had only weeks. But you have more now. Not immortality like you'd get for your—to the point." She had tilted the knife, so it was cutting a little deeper into his flesh. "Yes. Can't you be straightforward a little too?"

"No. This is making a point that I think you're going to remember for a very long time. You will won't you? Think about me cutting off your balls and dick, impressive as it is when you think to pull the same shit with other women." She smiled at him then. "You know, being an immortal without a dick will be pretty boring for you, don't you think? I mean, that does seem to be the only thing you're using to think with."

"I'm sorry." She asked him what he was sorry for. "Right now? Well, I'd have to say everything I've done since I was hatched. But mostly, right at this second, that I'd assumed having you healed would be a good thing."

She asked him if he'd healed her. It was Theo that answered her.

"We all have had a part in making sure you're around for a little while longer. If you'd let my brother go, we can sit here and have a nice talk. Or not. I don't really care so long as you understand that his dragon will come out soon if he feels threatened for too much longer." She looked at Finn and saw him there, the dragon in his eyes. "Jamie?"

"I'm okay now. I just was embarrassed in thinking that you were thinking I stank." She put her knives back after moving away from Finn. "I'm sorry. So, I can assume that since the other three shook their heads, I'm not a family member. How many more sniffs should I expect now? The next time you have something going on behind my back, you'd be safer to just tell me about it."

"I will. And just one more. Milo isn't in town just yet. I promise the rest of them will keep you in the loop from now on as well. And you are a part of this family. Since the moment you came here and fit in with us, you are a family member. You're not immortal—we didn't want to go that far—but your cancer isn't nearly as consuming as it had been. As it is, you'll still die, but you have more time to hang out with us." Jamie sat down and took her best friend's hand into hers. Pem had always been her friend. She'd only just realized how much the other woman had come to mean to her. "Would you like to be immortal? There will be magic as well. I don't know what it would entail. Pem can work with you on it if you'd like. You'll not die, not ever. You won't gain weight, have cancer ever again, nor will you be able to get anything else. There is one more brother. Milo. He's away at the moment working on a project for our parents. He has skills that can get them anything they need that the rest of them can't get."

"Such as?" He explained to her what they were needing. "I can do that as well. I'm not saying I hack into computers daily, but I can usually work around firewalls and such. That's not something I tell many people either." Theo said he'd keep that in mind. That perhaps she could work with Milo on projects. "I think I might like that. But for now, the twenty-million-dollar question is, do I want to be an immortal? Is it something I need to answer you about now?"

"Wait." She looked at Pem when she shouted. "Of course you want to be immortal. You need to be. If for no other reason than I want you around."

"That's sort of selfish, don't you think?" Pem asked her what she meant by that. "For yourself, not for me. Let me explain. I've not had a good life. I know that you've not either. However, if you really give it some thought, you'd say that no one has. You're in an amazing place right now. A great family, even though they're a little pushy. Money out the ass, and you have a roof over your head. I have, let me see—zip. Less than that, even. I don't even have a job, nor an offer—no place to live. Because as wonderful as it would be living in your home, we both know I'd have to take one of these idiots out, and that isn't going to be good for our friendship. I have to think about this."

"I could support you." Jamie knew that Pem was going to say that and just shook her head. "Yes, you'd no more like that than I would. I guess you're right. I don't like it, but you're right. This is your decision to make, and it will be a hard one. I think."

"It is." She looked back at Theo, and he smiled at her. "What? Do you have some point to make with that winking shit? So you know, happily married men aren't my cup of tea."

"Mine either." They all laughed, and she joined them. For some reason, she just wanted to be alone. When she stood up, so did the men. Jamie asked them if they had something to do too. "No. We were all around when men treated women with more respect. Also, if you make this decision to be immortal, you will have our support, in any form you'd want. And the job offer working with Milo? It still stands. I think we overwork him sometimes, looking for loopholes."

"I'll keep that in mind. I'm assuming I should wait on Milo. I know that some shifters are not the share and share alike kind of people." Theo told her they were a jealous sort, but not usually within the family. "Thanks for that. I do have shit I need to do today. Looking for a job is one of them. As I said, I can't live here forever. I do want my own space."

She didn't need to look for a job right away. As retired service personnel, she had some pension that she could fall back on. It wasn't a great deal, but she figured it would keep her in crackers with her soup.

It was a lovely day. As the nights were getting longer now, she knew it would be around nine before the sun went down. Walking along the streets, she thought about the offer they'd given her. Not just the job, but the immortality as well.

Ending up at the little park that had seen better days, she sat down on the stone walkway and began pulling weeds. She had always enjoyed the outdoors and working in a garden. Jamie couldn't remember the last time she'd been able to do anything like this. As she pulled weeds, she thought about her sister. The small nudge at her mind had her tensing up for some reason.

It's Carson Manning. I wanted you to know some things. I just found out that you left the house, or I wouldn't have been so forward and contacted you directly. Not that it matters now, but I do want to speak to you about your sister and the money. It is gone, but at no fault of anyone but your parents. Jamie asked her what they'd done. *You don't sound all that surprised. I'm guessing that, in addition to leaving you with a crap ton of shit to do, they also left a lot of things undone before leaving this earth.*

Pretty much. They were great at being starters of stuff but not very good at seeing things to the end. What did you figure out? By the way, if you're going to be anything like the sniffers I just left, they're not my mate. Carson laughed and told her she'd heard about that. *Sniffing me like I'm a tasty meal. Do you believe that shit?*

For them, I guess I should. However, I think they meant well. Jamie said she'd figured that out as well. *Anyway. When your parents set up so that your sister would have gotten care, they neglected to have someone add to the money. That's nothing to do with your insurance. The company that took care of the policy just did the same to the one you turned over to her, like not having it invested so there would be enough return on the money to keep growing. Or at the very least, caring for her.*

I don't understand. How did my parents set up some insurance money for her? She was hurt when they were killed. Carson was quiet for a few seconds. *I mean, I'm to understand that Pem's mother-in-law can see ghosts, but I doubt very much they would have been able to set up insurance.*

Jamie, did you know that your sister was born handicapped? The question and what it meant startled her. *Melissa was born with a brain injury. If she'd been born today, they would have been able to take care of it. But they didn't know what to do with it back then. I thought you might have known that.*

No. I mean, she was little, about five, when my parents were in the accident with her. I'm older than Missy by sixteen years. By the time she was born, I was already away from home and in college. I was a quick learner and reading well before I should have been. After that, I joined the service and rarely returned home. They'd started over, you see, and seemed to have no idea what to do with me. They weren't ignoring me, just I was older, and the baby was...I just realized how Mom was forever telling me that Missy was a handful. I just figured it was because they were both a lot older than they had been with me. Missy was a baby that was conceived while Mom was going through menopause.

That explains a great deal. And I can understand about having an older child and an infant. Some of the family has done that. Had a baby earlier in their marriage, then decided to have another one later. We're all immortal, and having children should we want is always an option. But there are so many rules now. Changes in how people think a child should be raised. It's not what I've done just so you know. I give them a steak in the yard and leave them there until they're old enough to care for themselves. They both laughed. Jamie knew that the Mannings would have been good parents.

Otherwise, the sniffers would have been terrible adults. Jamie did feel badly that she hadn't known about Missy. She wished that she'd taken better care of being a curious sister. *I've taken care that the money is being invested with some of the companies we're co-owners of. It'll be a good return for your sister.*

Thank you for that. What else? While I've never met you, I have a feeling you're working up to something else. Carson said she was a smart girl. *Yes. It's my looks that turn people off.*

Theo said that you were beautiful. I believe him. However, I don't want you to be freaked out — by the way, that's a term we use a great deal. Not freaking out. But anyway, right next to the roses nearby, you'll see a small creature. His name is Jangles. I have no idea who told him that would be a good name, but he's a good faerie. He would like to be yours.

I need a faerie? Carson said she did, simply to keep her safe as well as helping her being around a lot of dragons. *I see him. He's very…well, vibrating.*

Yes. They're full of energy. I wouldn't have pointed him out to you, but apparently, they have all been watching you clean out the weeds in the garden you're in. They need the flowers there, you see. She nodded, then remembered that Carson wasn't there. The little man flew up to sit on her knee. *Jangles will talk to you. And I don't know why this is, but once you accept him, you'll be able to understand him. He only speaks faerie.*

Perhaps because I'm not a Manning. Carson said that could be it. *I accept him as my friend. I need a friend more than I think I might need a faerie at this point in my life.*

If you say so. She wasn't sure what that meant, but let it go. *Also, I hope you don't mind, but I sent a crew of faeries to your family home to clean it up. The title of the home — I've found where you've been trying to get it in your name rather than yours and Missy's. It's only in your name. I've not seen it on the inside, but I know it's close to my nephews' homes. I wanted to buy it when we were looking for places that were for sale in that area, but the realtor told us that it was in probate. Are you planning to sell it?*

I don't know what I'm going to do now. I have been given a better outlook on life, you might say. Carson told her she was glad for that. *I'm thinking if it was good or not. But it is nice to know I have options.*

Jamie wasn't ready to go to the house just yet. She'd not been able to do much of anything because the deed had had both her and her sister's names on it. It wasn't left in a will, but the courts had set it up that way to save her, she supposed, from leaving her sister without anything. She didn't want to think about how she might well have done so ten years ago.

Finishing up the garden, she talked to Jangles. He was very well informed about the area, and she got caught up on all the happenings around town. Standing up, she decided she might as well go see what the old homestead looked like. Pulling out her phone, she told Pem what had happened and that she was going to stay there tonight so she could think.

"Good for you. Call me if you need anything. If there

are faeries there, you'll be all right. But be careful. I just got you back. I don't want to lose you again."

After hanging up, she and Jangles walked to the house. She'd forgotten how massive the sucker was.

~*~

He was glad Jamie had called him and Pem to meet her at the house. Not that she was afraid of anything that might be in there, but she had said she wanted to bounce some things around. Theo could understand that, as well. She'd been tossed a great deal today.

As soon as he walked into the front hall, Theo could see her living there with Milo. There wasn't any reason for him to think that Milo was her mate. He wouldn't be back for a few more days. But the image, so detailed, of the two of them having Thanksgiving here made him want to call his brother home right now and have him meet her.

"This house has been in my family for generations. As you can tell, no one has done much in the way of updating anything in all that time. I think the faeries did a great job on the wallpaper in here, but I think the old flocked wallpaper went out about the time my parents were born." Pem ran her hand over the remaining ugly paper and shivered. Jamie laughed. "Yes, I used to have that same reaction when I was a kid. Nasty shit."

The house was in surprisingly good condition. Asking her when was the last time she'd been there, Jamie told him it had been about the time her parents had been killed. About eight years now.

"Even then, I didn't stay all that long. They'd had all their arrangements taken care of, so all I had to do was come here and take care of the will. I just found out that Missy, my sister, has been handicapped since she was born." Theo could tell she was upset about that. However, it was Pem that asked her about it. "I wasn't home much after she was born. I would call home, or they'd call me, but we rarely talked about anything personal. As I said to Carson, they weren't terrible parents, just not very close to me. I guess now that I know, it had a lot to do with Missy being a lot of trouble for them. I didn't have any idea, and I feel bad for it."

"They could easily have told you about how much they were having a hard time of it. I knew your parents, Jamie. They were cold. I think that it had more to do with them being only children of only children. They didn't know how to act around two children." Jamie smiled at Pem and told her she was more than likely right as the two of them moved to another room. "I know I am. You move in here, and the two of us will have such a wonderful time of it."

"I can fix it up for the mistress." Jangles was riding on Theo's shoulder now and hanging tightly onto his ear. "I know she's going to fit in with the family, so it would be our pleasure to have this fixed up with what I see in her mind."

Theo thought about what she'd said to them earlier about keeping her informed about things. "All right, Jangles, but just this room. If she has what she wants in mind, she might not be so upset with me when I tell her that I okayed it." He nodded. "Jangles, just what you see in her mind. Nothing more. If you mess this up, she might well tell you that you've overstepped your bounds or something."

He nodded and moved into the room. Theo looked up to where he'd gone and saw that the faeries were there in full force. Shaking his head at how they were all so ready to do something for the young woman, he wondered if he'd be in a great deal of trouble with her or if she would be all right with it. Especially if it was just what she wanted.

Pem was in the kitchen with Jamie when he caught up with them. He could hear the buzz of the wings moving in the other room and wondered what they were up to. The room wasn't that bad, but he could see that it was out of date. The kitchen, however, was in terrible shape. It hadn't been updated in decades, he'd bet.

"The Darkhouse family didn't get rich by spending money needlessly. If it couldn't be fixed at all, then they'd get a replacement. You do notice that I didn't say new. I've never even had a new car. I drove around the one that my mom learned to drive in." Theo laughed and told her he knew someone that could fix this for her. "I was thinking of that. Either way, if I sell or live here, it's going to need to be updated a great deal. Especially this room. I wonder how they were able to keep staff with a stove that had to have wood put in it to use?"

"The faeries are working in the parlor. That is what

the room we were in is called." Jamie asked him what he meant. "They're very powerful. When they're together and have something to do, they're amazing. Jangles wanted to do something nice for you, and I okayed it. If you don't like it, it's completely my fault. I said he could do only the room we had been in."

"I still don't understand." He told her she might understand it better if she were to go back to the parlor. "All right. Is this going to make me have to kick your ass?"

"Christ, I hope not. I like you." Pem went with Jamie, and he knew the exact moment Jamie entered the room. Her cries of delight were just what he wanted to hear. He entered the room just as Pem was holding her friend. "I thought you liked it. I'm so sorry if you don't. He said you had in your head what you wanted this room to— it's very beautiful in here. I love the colors."

"Me too." Jamie hugged him. "You have no idea how much I've dreamt of this room looking just like this. The wallpaper being gone alone would have made me happy, but this?" She shook her head and looked around. "Theo, this is absolutely what I wanted."

He really did love it too. Gone were the heavy couches that faced each other. The soft fabric ones that were there now looked inviting. Soft too. The fireplace was still the same. However, the marble had been deep cleaned, and it was pink, not the brown he'd thought it was.

The pictures that had been on the wall had been replaced with nature scenes. Places he'd bet Jamie had visited on her own. Over the mantel was a painting he'd seen in a large museum if it was the artist he thought it was. He moved closer to see that it was indeed from a very famous painter.

Other things had been added to the room too — tables with flowers on them. Theo especially loved that the curtains, heavy ones that let in no light, were gone, replaced by wooden blinds that were open to let it the beautiful scenery of the gardens and yards beyond.

Jangles was now with Jamie, telling her he'd love to do the rest of the house for her. As they moved out of the parlor, he noticed there wasn't a television in this room. Nor did he see any kind of computer. Good. This would be a relaxing room for the two of them.

"Milo will live here with her, won't he?" Theo told Pem that he had seen it. "Me too. He was coming down the stairs with a holiday sweater on and holding a child's hand. It was so clear I thought that he'd beat us here today."

"I'm not going to tell either of them." Pem told him that might be a good idea. "I have them on occasion. But the faeries are going to make this house just the way the two of them like it. I have a feeling that Milo and Jamie are more alike in this than any of the rest of us are."

She moved to the wall where she'd touched the paper before going with her friend. Pem stood there for several moments before she turned to look at him. He didn't know what she was thinking about, but it hurt him on so many levels that she looked so very sad just now.

"I didn't know she was ill. She told me she'd found out about her cancer about a week before I was sent home." Theo told her he was sorry. "I am as well. I could have been there for her."

"Maybe you would have, but perhaps she had it in her mind not to tell you so you'd not be any different to her than you had been." Pem asked him what he meant. "She didn't want your pity. She wanted you just the way you are. As her best friend, that would be there no matter what."

"You think so?" Theo told her he'd want that for himself if he were to have something like Jamie did. "I never thought about it that way. I would have too. Treated her differently. I'd have hurt for her. As it was, we had so much fun while together. She could pull me out of my depression better than most. Plus, she would hug me unconditionally until I had what I needed from her."

"That's just what she wanted from you as well." Theo wasn't sure, but he thought Jamie wouldn't have told her friend for fear of making her more depressed. Both women had had a rough life, as Jamie had pointed out. Now he could only see good things coming to them. "Something just occurred to me. Jamie said she didn't have any money or a place to live. I did hear from Aunt Carson about how she'd fixed up the house title for her. But the Darkhouses, they had a great deal of money, didn't they?"

"They did. I didn't." Theo said he was sorry for

talking behind her back. "No worries. But you have to come and see the kitchen. It's unbelievable how amazing they made it look."

She told him that her parents had left the money in a reserve for her and her sister. "To care for her, you mean?" Jamie said that was it. "Do you have any idea how much that is? I mean, Aunt Carson told me. It's been converted to your name, as it should have been years ago."

"When I left here, there was a fat argument. They told me I wasn't to get a dime. I didn't bother the money, even though it was still in the will that I got it. I don't believe I was ever told how much there was." Theo told her there was still a great deal of it. "Do you think I need to know the amount? I mean, will it be enough to keep me from having to work if I don't want to? I'm not being a bitch right now, but I've been thrown a great deal today. Don't you agree?"

"I understand, I do. Like I said, it's all yours now. The insurance that my aunt fixed for you is much more than Missy will need. Aunt Carson also made it so that you could collect the rest of the things they left behind. All of it is now in your name." Jamie asked him if it was a lot. "Yes. Even by our standards, being very wealthy, you're a billionaire several times over, Jamie. A few of the stocks you own are older than a few of the investments that my family has. You were what most would call born rich." He laughed. "Christ, you could own this state if you wished."

"My parents were tight fisted with their things. I

guess I'm very lucky about that." She looked around the room, then back at him. "I'd like to be immortal. I'd like to live in this home for the rest of my days. If you'd not mind the faeries fixing the rest of it for me."

"I'm glad to hear that." He kissed her on the cheek. "You and Jangles work out what you want, and I'm sure that in no time at all, this place will be the showplace that it was always meant to be. I'm so very glad you're going to be a part of this family."

He'd bet that by the time he was back at his own home, this place would be finished up. Jamie had been thinking of this house for most of her life. It would be just like she wanted it, and Theo knew that Milo was going to love living there. He'd not been very happy with the home that had been bought for him. Perhaps they'd work on something about it as well.

Theo and Pem helped her with the rooms in that they made sure the faeries understood not to go overboard with the revamping of the house. On his way out the door, he noticed that someone had set the faeries onto the grounds. Yes, Theo thought, this place was going to be a grand showcase in no time.

Chapter 9

Sandra hated to wait for her turn. The system sucked in the way they did things around here. She thought that if a person had money, they shouldn't have to wait in line for anything. Even in alphabetical order was stupid. Merkel would put her at the end of the line somewhere, and she didn't think being in that slot was going to do her the least bit of good.

The judge already looked pissed off. She stood up and waited for him to notice her. It didn't take him long. When he put down his gavel, something she thought he should use on a few heads instead of the desk, he looked at her with a meaner look than he'd had before.

"Ms. Merkel. Either sit down, or I'm going to null and void your question session with me and send you back to jail. I've got a full docket today, and you're just adding to it. Sit down and shut your mouth until I—"

"I don't want to sit down. I only have a single question." He waved at her, and she decided he meant for her to go on. "I want you to release me for a few days.

A week would be all right with me. Two would make it better. I heard that they reopened Merkle's Mark, and I didn't authorize it. I need to go there and see what they've done."

"You want me to just release you. To say, hey, go ahead and see to your life while the rest of the inmates have to wait until such time as they're released, or they've made arrangements to have someone do whatever it is for them. Is that what you're asking me?" Sandra told him she'd return when she was finished knocking some heads around. "I see. And this knocking heads around? I'm assuming you know just who that might entail?"

"My husband and his supposed sister." She did the quote thing around supposed and thought by now the judge would have figured out what she felt about Rachel being Chad's sister. "They're plotting again, and I won't have it. It's bad enough that you keep telling me I have no job and no home. If you let me do this thing with them, I'll come back and not bother you again."

"It might well be worth it just to make it so you can't bother me again. You say two weeks will do it, do you? I'm supposing you'll need some money for this head knocking event. Correct? How much would you need? A few hundred?" This was working out better than she could have hoped. Sandra told him she'd need at the very least a few thousand. "Of course. I'm guessing that head knocking has gotten a bit more expensive than I remember it."

She didn't understand what he was saying. Sandra

was sure he was either missing the point, or he had a sense of humor she didn't understand. Asking him if he was going to give her the money and the time, she waited for him to answer. The man was entirely too stressed, she thought when he rubbed his hands through his hair and over his face several times as he looked in her direction.

"Ms. Merkle, you do understand that you're in jail for murder. Also, you have no assets. No restaurant. No home. And as I can understand this need entirely, having spent time with you, you have no husband." She told him that remained to be seen. "Yes, well, that's neither here nor there. You're in jail until such time as you have a trial. Murder is a crime, and we citizens take that one very seriously. I have no idea why you think you should be able to just leave here for a few days to a couple of weeks. This is not a system that lets people out to knock heads together. The law states, and I've gone over this with you several times, that—" She told him she had money. "Do not interrupt me again. I'm in charge here, and the sooner you understand that, the better off you're going to be. You're going to be sent back to your cell, with a word to your keepers that you're not to come back here, bother me, or even to request anything until your court date."

"Then you tell me how I'm supposed to be in here and running my restaurant at the same time? There are things going on that you're just too stupid to understand. I swear. Did you get your judgeship from a bubblegum machine?" He just stared at her, his eyes wide in shock.

"I can see you're disbelieving that I'm smarter than you. It's true that I'm smarter than most of the people in this room. Even if you were to put all their brain cells together with yours, you'd see that I'm telling you like it is. You have to do something about this, or I'm going to take matters into my own hands regarding your inability to see reason."

"Did you just threaten me?" She said he could take it any way he wanted, but she was getting out of there today. "I see."

When he turned to the police in the room with them, he put his hand over the microphone on his desk. He spoke to them for a good ten minutes while she just stood there. Sandra didn't know why he had a microphone up there in the first place. He was forever yelling at people.

The police came toward her with their hands on their guns. As they spread out around the room, she wondered what the hell was going on now. Didn't these people have better things to do than to act like they were bad assed? Sandra could take them on all by herself if they didn't have her chained up like some sort of animal.

"Ms. Merkel, you're under arrest for threatening a sitting judge. Come with us quietly, and we won't have to hurt you." She snorted at the man talking. "Are you going to be nice and come with us?"

"What is it you're planning to do to me, and I'll tell you if I'm going to be nice or not. I don't have time for this— Did you just say you were arresting me? You do see that I'm already a prisoner in this town. What is it you think you're going to do? Add more time on my staying in that outrageous cell?" He told her again that she was under arrest and started reading her rights to her. "Oh, for Christ's sake. I'm not going anywhere with you idiots until this thing with the supreme chump up there has been taken care of. I think you all have come from the same gene pool. I want the fuck out of here now."

They leapt at her. Perhaps that wasn't right, but they did all converge on her at once. Even as she fought to get away from them, her chain kept tangling her up, and she was falling down with each movement to stand up. Finally, all movement stopped, and Sandra had one of the cops wrapped around the neck with her chains.

"You need to let him go." She moved to tighten the grip she had on the cop's neck. "Ms. Merkel, I'm going to shoot you if you don't allow him to be released. You're forcing my hand in this."

"I'm forcing your hand? What about my hand? You jumped me, not the other way around. Undo this monstrosity of chains from my hands and ankles, and I'll let him go." She wasn't stupid enough to think they were going to just let her get up and leave, but she was in charge this time, and she loved every second of it. "I don't want to have to hurt him anymore, but you're going to do what I say, or he'll die, and it'll be your fault. I want to get out of here to make sure my business isn't failing. That's all I want."

"All you're going to get is a longer prison term if you kill that man. And if you do, you can be assured that I'm going to kill you." She asked him if he was threatening her. That the judge got all nasty when she did it. "I'm not threatening you. I'm telling you what is going to happen. We don't take kindly to having our officers killed. We've had enough of that for several lifetimes if you ask me."

She moved. It was only to release the pressure on her leg, but the loud snap had her thinking she'd broken something. It didn't feel painful, but all the same, she had them just where she wanted them. Then she was falling down a deep dark hole.

There were a woman and a man sitting on a couch when she opened her eyes, talking to someone, a person she didn't see. In fact, she didn't know where she was or how she'd gotten there. As she looked around, she realized the woman was ignoring her, sitting next to a man that looked at her with a sickly smile. Who were they, these people? What was her own name, for that matter? Turning back to the couple, she realized they were now staring at her.

"Where am I?" The man, a person she didn't know, but on some level knew he was in charge, smiled at her. He asked her the last thing she remembered. "What the hell sort of question is that? If I knew that, I'd have an idea where I am. Christ, is everyone stupid except for me?"

"I know the answer to that as well, but I'm not going to tell you until you start to cooperate. I will tell you that I'm so very happy to see you here at this time. It does my heart good to know that something happened." He was talking in riddles, and she asked him to tell her who he was. "You know me. You know my wife as well. That was put into your memory the moment you opened your eyes.

"Xavier. Your name is Xavier. Her name is Cindi." She hadn't any idea why their names were there when she didn't even remember her own name. "How did I get here?"

"You came here because it was here that you were meant to be. It's all in the rules that are now in your memory. What's your name? Do you remember that?" She shook her head, then remembered something. She asked him that. "Yes. You're Merkle, but that's not your first name. What is it?"

"Sandra. My name is Sandra Merkle." She thought about the chains she was remembering and looked down at her wrists and legs. "They finally got their shit together, it looks like. I'm finally fucking free."

"Sort of." Cindi stood up and asked the man if he wanted anything to munch on before supper. That couldn't be right. She'd been in the courthouse early in the day. "It's the tenth of August. It's been several days since you were in the courthouse."

"No. No. It was the end of July. I had to stay—I was staying someplace I didn't want to be." Her head was pounding, and she asked the man if he had anything she could take for it. Then she remembered something else. "Chad. He's my husband. He's somewhere around here. I want you to find him for me so I can tell him something."

"I can tell him what you want. However, he's not going to come here. You're in no shape to have any conversation with him that will make him feel any better than he does at this time. You really did screw up."

Not remembering her name had been something she didn't like, and now that she remembered it, she thought she should also be able to remember what had brought her here. She looked at the man again and saw that the woman had returned and that they were both in different outfits. Something was going on, and she didn't care for it.

"You're back." She asked him what he meant. "Since you've not been able to recall enough to know your circumstances, I'll tell you the date again. This is August twenty-fifth."

"What are you talking about? There is no way I've been here that long." He told her she'd left and had returned. It was exhausting for her to be there with them. "Why am I with you, anyway? I don't know anything about you."

"You've been making your way to us since July twentieth." The date. It rattled around in her head, and she wondered about it. "Until you come to the realization as to why you're here, you're going to keep coming back. As soon as you do, however, I'm going to send you on."

"Send me on." It wasn't a question she said to him, but he told her that was what she had done to herself. "I don't know what I'm doing here. This is the stupidest thing I've ever done. Tell me what I'm doing here, and

I want you to have Chad come here. There is no reason whatsoever why he'd not come to see me now that I'm free."

"Chad is here. When we last spoke, I told him you were coming here. He said he had a few things to say to you. Would you like for me to call him?" Sandra was afraid for him to call Chad, but Xavier yelled out Chad's name, and he came into the room. Christ, what the fuck had he done to himself? "He's been walking a great deal. Getting to know the people in the town. Being relaxed has been good for him. And he's happy. Something that he rarely got around you. Also, he's having a wonderful time working for my family. He's here. Talk to him."

"What am I doing here?" The woman repeated what she'd said to Chad. "What the hell are you doing that for? He can hear me just fine. Why don't the two of you go away so I can have a real conversation with him? Now. I don't have time to fuck around with the two of you and Chad today. I have shit to do. I want you out—"

Something rushed at her head, like all the memories that she needed to know were suddenly just there. Her name was Sandra. Sandra Merkle. There was a restaurant named for her. A home that she had burnt up. Sitting down on the floor, the only thing she could seem to get close to, Sandra let the memories of her having a chain around one of the cops, and something hit her hard in the head.

"They did something to me. The cops. That's why I'm confused. They hit me with something. I was holding the cop in the chain, and then I woke up here." She could understand why she was, but she refused to acknowledge it. "You people. You're the death watchers. You have something to do with the dead. I'm not dead."

"You are, as a matter of fact. Have been for over a month. We wondered if you'd remember being shot. But you were. When you broke the neck of the officer you were holding hostage, you were shot six times by the other officers. Overkill, but worth it, I believe the paper said about you being dead." Chad sat down next to the couple. She looked at him while Xavier filled in the blank spaces as to what had happened up until she'd come here. "You were cremated the day after you were killed. I think that is why you took so long to find us. You didn't want to believe you were dead."

"I'm not dead, damn it. I'm as living as you are." She knew on some level that she needed to take care with this man and woman. That they could and would send her away, what they had told her they would do before. "I'll show you that I'm not dead."

Getting up, she made her way to Chad. He didn't move when she kicked out at him, but she did fall on her ass. Cindi told Chad what was going on, and he laughed. At her. Standing up again, she paused when Xavier said her full name.

"You will cease and desist in this now." She couldn't move, not even to blink. When he told her to look at him, her entire body turned to the man without her having any control over it. "For the crimes against you, I sentence you to the white room. You will stay there for a period of ten thousand years. Leave."

The room she was in was white. Laughing, she told herself that was why it was called that. Looking around, she wondered what she was supposed to do there. There wasn't a window she could look out. Not any kind of television she could turn on. It was then that Sandra realized there wasn't any sound. Not of her breathing, her heart beating, or a slight breeze to make her feel welcome in the room.

"Hello?" She wandered around but had no idea if she was getting anywhere. "All right. You've had your fun with me. I'll try and be good."

Nothing. Not an echo even. Sandra had a feeling that when he told her ten thousand years, he meant just that. She sat down. Suddenly a wall was behind her, and she leaned into it. Something was wrong with this place, and someone was going to pay for her being here.

"Hello? Where the fuck are you? Come here right now and take me back." She thought she'd prefer dead over whatever this was. "You fucking bastards. I'm not kidding. I want out of here."

No one came to her. Sandra knew she should have gotten more information. Like how long ten thousand years was. A calendar appeared on the floor. A clock as well. Now that she had a date and time, she wished she didn't. Time, it seemed, was mocking her.

"Christ, what am I going to do now?"

~*~

Jamie sat on the lounger and soaked up some sun. It had rained all day yesterday, and she'd not been able to go out on her deck. The faeries had done such a wonderful job on the house that she had no memories of the place it had been before. It was the best thing that could have happened to her of late.

"What's up?" Sitting up just enough to make out the person that had spoken, Jamie invited Pem to join her. They'd been getting together at least once a day, on the phone or in person. Pem came up on the deck and sat down in one of her new chairs she'd purchased. "Oh, this is really nice. I might have to learn where you got it. It's comfy."

"Thanks. What is wrong?" She asked her what she meant. "I mean, what is wrong? Something is up. You usually have something chipper to say to me, and today, you're talking about lawn furniture. So, tell me what's happened."

"My dad is out. He's been released so he can get himself an attorney. I'm worried for Uncle Austin and Grandma. Not so much me. I'm with a dragon, but I still don't want him to hurt me." Jamie told her she didn't want that either. "With Sandra out of their hair, they're still tense, and it's because of my family issues."

"Yeah, I know that too. I was told no less than five times that I'm not to let my guard down for any reason. That Patrick is coming." Jamie watched her dearest friend. "I've also heard that Milo is coming back soon."

"Is he?" Pem turned and looked at her. "I thought he

was going to be gone for a few more days. Theo will be happy. The two of them are close. Are you going to take the job working with him?"

"I thought about it. For now, I'm going to get my shit together and sort of chill out. I go to the doctor tomorrow, and I'm excited about that. Also, I've been told by the bank that my estate money is now available to me. That family that you're related to sure has a lot of pull." Pem told her that they were more connected than even she knew about. "I'm going to see my sister tonight. Would you like to go with me? I know you don't know her, but I'd be happy for the company."

"I'd love to do that." Jamie looked out over her back yard when Pem did. "Can you believe this view? I mean, when you talked about this place, it never seemed like a place that I'd want to visit with you. But since you've gotten it just the way you want it, I think I could come here daily. How are you and Jangles working out?"

"He's perfect. Not a talker, though he can be when he thinks of something. I like the fact that he can run errands I don't even know how to begin. Did I tell you that he was able to get my computer and Internet set up? I was going to do it, but he just moved in and did it. I think he's liking that I'm being relaxed. I am too." The two of them laughed, and she wondered more about Patrick. "What do you think your father is going to do to you, Pem? He's broke, right?"

"Yes. Grandma and I have been talking about that too. What he might do if he were to come around. With all of us being immortal, I don't know what he thinks he can do by way of hurting us. Or, for that matter, what he thinks he can demand of us." Jamie asked her if she thought he'd thought of that. "Likely no. I'd say he's only thinking of what his needs are, and fuck everyone else around the place. But then, he's always had it in his head that he's the only person in the world that should be getting everything he wants."

"I saw your uncle the other day. Austin is looked better. I know he had a pretty rough time of it for a while, but he seems to be making great strides in winning over the people here." Pem told her that he mostly worked the back kitchen of the pizza place, but he was having a wonderful time of it. "Who would have thought a man like him would go so low to be able to regroup and start over? I know it is because of his family that he's trying so hard, but the man is like a new person from what he was when I met him that one time five or so years ago."

"Every day, he's different." Pem leaned back on her chair and closed her eyes.

It was then that Jamie looked out over her back yard. The glint of something startled her. No one was allowed access to her yard as far as she knew. Not saying anything to Pem, she reached out to Jangles.

See what that might be for me. Will you? After pointing to the area, she knew that whatever it had been had moved. The glint of something shiny was closer now. *Jangles. Go and find one of the dragons for me. I think we're about to have some trouble.*

The shot to her house had Jamie pulling Pem down off her chair and to the decking. The two of them hid behind the hot tub that had been delivered just yesterday while she tried her best to get her bearings. Even before she could explain to Theo what was going on when he reached out to her, Pem was jerked from where they were, and Patrick had a gun to her head. Jamie pulled her own gun out from behind her, where it was stuck in her pants, and pointed it at the man.

"Where is the money, Pem? I know you have it all." He was pulling Pem away from Jamie as he spoke. "Get me the money, or I'm going to kill you both."

"I don't have any money." Pem looked at her. *I'm an immortal — the same as you are. Nothing can hurt me, Jamie. Remember that?*

She did remember that but had no idea what she was saying. It wasn't until one of the dragons landed in the yard that it occurred to her what her friend was saying. She asked her where she should shoot.

It won't matter. But he can't get away with me. Your house would suffer badly when the dragons kill him, I think.

The big dragon was making his way toward them, his body as red as the blood that was making its way down Pem's cheek from the gun being rammed into her skin. Patrick started yelling about money and blood. Before she could lose her house to dragon fire, Jamie fired twice.

The first bullet hit Pem in the shoulder. Jamie knew for a fact that it wouldn't kill her, even if she wasn't immortal. The second shot hit Patrick right between the eyes. As he fell back, he fired once, and the bullet went wild.

The dragon stopped moving, and she was glad for it. Dizzy now, she fell back into one of the chairs she'd only just gotten put together instead of sitting. Finn asked her several times if she was all right before she leaned over and puked in the grass beyond her decking. Looking up, she saw that Pem was being looked at and that Theo was standing close to her.

"Are you really a red dragon?" Finn said he was. "Would you have burnt my house if you'd hit Patrick?"

"Yes. More than likely. I would have rebuilt for you, but he would have been just as dead and gone. Are you all right, Jamie?" She said she thought she was. "You've been shot. Did you know that? The bullet entered your head. Are you sure you're all right?"

"I didn't know." Putting her fingers to her forehead, she felt the tender wound there. As she was trying to figure out if she was hurting, the bullet fell into her hand, and she stared at it. Holding it out to Finn, she asked him if that was natural to have it fall out like that.

"I have no idea. I'd say it is, but who the fuck knows? If you're really all right, I'm going to see to Pem now. You just sit here until I can get my own heart to stop pounding. And I'd let Pem hold you as much as she wants. She's freaked out." She nodded and stopped when it hurt. "Theo, can you see to Jamie now? She needs Pem too after I make sure she's going to be fine."

Pem hugged her several times before she finally let

her go. There was blood on them both, but neither of them seemed too terribly concerned about it. Jamie asked her friend if she was all right.

"I am now. I thought for sure that you were going to die when I saw where that bullet went. The fucker shot you after he was dead." Jamie couldn't help it; she laughed. "I don't think that's the least bit funny, Jamie. You could have been killed."

"You were the one that told me that we were immortal and to shoot." She said she had no idea that Patrick would shoot after she'd shot him. "Must have been a muscle contraction that had him firing. It happens sometimes."

"It happens sometimes. Just like that, you're all right with him shooting you after he was dead." Jamie shrugged and watched Pem. "You're taking this very well, you know. I'm worried that you're going to be a basket case later."

"I won't be. He's gone now, and we're both all right. No more stress. All right?" Pem looked over to where Patrick's body still lay. "No. Don't look at him. Don't feel sorry that he's dead. Move on and up, Pem, the way we need to. You helped me save our lives, and I'll never forget that. Thank you."

"You saved my life too." Pem hugged her tightly and looked into her face. "I can never thank you enough for pulling me away from being shot. Grandma will be so happy he's gone. I think Uncle Austin will as well."

Theo smiled at her. "I thank you as well. When Jangles came to us when we were in the barn, I thought for sure I was going to get to take him out. Thank you for saving the day, Jamie. I owe you as well."

After Patrick's body was taken away, she sat where she was. The pack was going to put him on their land and let him be eaten by the scavengers. There were policemen on the force that were part of the pack, and in a few days, probably more like a month, they were going to have someone call in that they'd found his body. By then, she'd bet his skull would have found itself in some deep hole or in an animal's den. Patrick would be considered a suicide. All would be well.

"Come and have dinner with us." She stared up at George, the only brother she was talking to very much. "I'll even pay. Think of it as a way to pay you back for killing a monster."

"You think you buying me a steak dinner will be enough payment for killing Patrick?" George asked her if she thought so as well. "Yes. I guess I do. And dinner sounds wonderful. Just not steak. Not yet. I need something less bloody for now."

He was still laughing as they loaded up in his car. Dover was going with them, as was Hadley. They were good guys to be around, and she found herself laughing more than not. These people were going to be all right to be around, she thought. All right, indeed.

Chapter 10

George and Theo were at the airport when the plane landed. They'd gotten breakfast together, then had gone to a craft store to pick up some things to make some embarrassing signs to welcome their brother home. Sure, he'd only been gone for a few days, but the three of them were closer than the rest of them. As soon as Theo saw his brother, the signs were discarded, and he and George rushed to their brother.

"What's happened?" Milo told them to just get him home. "Sure. But you're going to tell us why you look as if you've lost everything. Did someone hurt you, Milo? Where are they? Are they still here at the airport?"

Theo was looking around and missed that his brother had stopped moving. Going back to him, he told him he was sorry. George was asking him again what they needed to help him with. Milo said he just wanted to go home. That he was exhausted.

He must have been. No sooner had they gotten his luggage from the jet and Milo into the car than he was sound asleep. They'd planned to spend the day with him, getting lunch with him and hooking up sometime during the day with Jamie, in order to see if the two of them were mates. But this seemed serious enough that Theo debated telling his mom.

I know he's tired. Theo hadn't been so relieved to hear his mom's voice as he was in that second. *I spoke to him on the plane. The poor boy has been working double shifts for us in getting some information, and he's worn out. Nothing more, just exhausted.*

I've never seen him like this before. For that matter, anyone. She said she'd told him to rest up, but he was stubborn. *Yes. I wonder who he might have gotten that from?*

Not me. Theo laughed and told George what Mom had said. He thought that Milo was stubborn, but Mom was ten times worse. *Anyway. If you're finished insulting your mother, I'd like for you to get him home and into his bed. Anything you were planning with him can wait until he can enjoy it more. Also, it might be a good time to take Jamie over to see him. While he's out. It might be sneaky, but you'd have an answer. I want one, too, as a matter of fact.*

He didn't feel good about that, but his mom was right. They'd all know and could move on to the next phase, whatever that would be. Theo did think that Milo could use a mate, if for no other reason than for him to get laid. Also, she'd be there to make sure he didn't overwork himself like Milo tended to do.

Stopping by Jamie's house seemed to be the best course of action. While he didn't want to wake Milo to have him sniff her, George had pointed out that if she were his mate, she could take him into her home instead of them taking him across town to his own. Where someone would have to be there all the time.

"I can tell you don't have a mate." George asked him what that was supposed to mean. "You wouldn't dream of saying something that selfish to your own mate."

"What the hell does that mean?" Theo told him. "Oh. Well, I suppose I was being selfish, and it was a little sexist of me to want to pawn our brother off on a woman. I didn't think of it as it being her duty, but I did want to have him well cared for. I guess I need to work on that, being a better male when it comes to what I think a woman should be doing."

"You don't have to if you want to have the shit knocked out of you by your mate." George asked him if he thought his mate would be a ball cruncher. "Have you met any of the Manning women, George? I mean, there isn't a timid one in the bunch. That goes for our mates too. I'd not want to take on any of them. And work very hard in keeping on their good side. Related or not, I think they'd find a way to have me fall from a great height and let me lay there until I healed."

They pulled into the driveway of Jamie's home. It was something, this home that she'd just had updated. It was larger than his by a great deal, and even Finn's home was small by comparison. She was sitting on the front porch, rocking in what appeared to be like one of the swings his parents had at their home when he'd been younger.

"I think I might have run off Jangles. He was here for a little while this morning but decided I'm going to have to find me something to do." Jamie laughed. "I've been getting my recertification to work in the new hospital. What are you guys up to?"

"We've brought Milo over to see if he's your mate." Theo looked at George and wondered if the guy would ever find a way to ease into a conversation. He was entirely too blunt and honest right from the start. "Mom said you might be able to tell, and then we'd all know."

"You're not getting on my good side, George." He asked her why not. "Because this isn't how I wanted to start my day off. I was going to take a walk. Then maybe go into town and have some lunch. I don't think I've ever eaten a meal out on my own before. Now you two show up with my potential mate and fucking ruin my day."

"I'm sorry, Jamie." She looked over at Theo as he told George to get back in his car. "I don't know what we were thinking. Milo is going to rest up for a little while, and he'll see you when he sees you. I'm sorry."

"How does this work?" Theo asked her if she wanted to see too. "I do. I don't know what it might mean for me, or him for that matter, but I'd like to know. Since you're here already. Will he wake up if I'm his mate?"

"Honestly? I haven't any idea. Mom didn't give us any details when we spoke to her about it. She just said to come by and see if you might be his mate. You don't have to do this." She told him she knew that. "All right.

I guess you'd have to do the sniffing thing. I know you hate that, but I really don't have any other idea on how we need to check."

Leaning into the back seat where Milo was sleeping, she stood up. The look on her face was pure confusion. When she didn't say anything, he didn't either. However, George didn't have the filter that he would hopefully get when he found his own mate.

"Are you?" She looked at his brother, then looked at him. "You're teasing us, aren't you? That's good that you can have a sense of humor about this. I know that when my mate comes along, I'm going to dazzle her—"

"Hush." George snapped his mouth closed with an audible click. Jamie looked at Theo before she spoke again. "He smells funny. I don't know what it is, but it's like he's ill. I haven't any idea why, but he smells of old blood."

"Old blood or iron?" She asked if there was a difference in the smells. "I don't know the answer to that, but Milo isn't a dragon. I didn't think iron would kill him any more than it would any of us, but if you smell it, that's something we need to have checked out. I'm going to call Winnie here. She's the protector, and she might be able to help with what it is you're detecting on him."

Winnie appeared just as he finished telling her what was going on. She asked him a couple of questions that he didn't know the answer to. He and George were told to take Milo into the house, and Theo was surprised when Jamie was all right with that. She enjoyed her alone time more than any person he knew.

"I smell iron too. Not a great deal of it, but he's sick with it. I doubt that he'd die from it, but it has affected him." She put her hand on his belly then up around his chest. "It's here. Surrounding his heart. After I take it out, I'm going to leave here to make sure I find the person responsible for this. All right? That means you'll have to wait for questions from me. If you have any, now would be the time to tell me."

"Is he my mate?" Theo watched Winnie as she seemed to struggle with answering Jamie. "I mean, all I could smell on him was the iron, as it turns out. If you can figure that out, I'd like to be made aware of it now."

"Much like you, I can't focus on anything but his illness. Trust me when I tell you, it will become clearer in the days ahead. Can he stay here? His faerie will be with him. If it's too much of a burden for you—"

"No. I want him to stay here. For no other reason than that, I owe this family my life, and I will do anything needed of me to take care of one of their own." Winnie nodded, then asked if she had any more questions. "Just one more. No biggie, but if he is my mate, will I have to worry about iron too?"

"Yes."

Winnie turned back to Milo. The bed he was lying on was perfect for his size. Whoever made the bedroom suite for this room had kept in mind that all of the Mannings were larger than life. Milo was the shortest at six foot ten inches.

Winnie didn't strain or anything like that when the iron that had been in his brother's body was pulled free. As soon as she put Milo into a deeper sleep, she told them, she disappeared, taking what appeared to be about a cup of iron in small, almost powered particles. Lily, Milo's faerie, knocked at the window, and it was Jamie that let her in.

"Whatever you need, you tell me, and I'll make sure you have it." Lily told her thanks and went to her master. "I'm assuming he's going to sleep for a little while. I'll be around if you need me."

Jamie just left them there. Theo looked at his brother, then at George. Neither of them seemed to understand what had just happened. Was she mad at them? Did she not want him in her house now?

Instead of standing around without answers, Theo went to find her. She was the closest thing he'd had to a sister, excluding Rachel, and he didn't want her upset with them. He found her in the kitchen.

"I'm going to have some cookies and tea. Would you like some?" He told her that would be good. "I'm going to talk, but so you know, I don't want you to answer. I'm just babbling right now, and if I don't, my head is going to explode. All right?"

"Yes. However, if I can answer, do you want me to?" She shook her head as she put a kettle on the burner to make some tea. "You do need to sit down, Jamie. I can hear your heart beating very quickly, and I don't want you stressed out. Just have a seat, and I'll make us the tea while you babble."

She sat down but played with the cup and saucer she'd been holding. He pulled the kettle off the burner then put his hand on it. In a shorter time than it would have taken the stove, he had hot water. Pouring them both a cup and finding her stash of scones, he sat down across from her. She stared at him for several moments before she spoke.

"I'm not going to lie to you when I tell you I'm terrified of becoming a mate to any of you." He asked her why. "I've come from a long line of people with mental illness. When I went to visit Missy yesterday, the doctor told me her illness is hereditary. It's like a missing gene, he told me. That it more than likely would make it so that if I were to have two children, one of them would be affected by it."

"No, not anymore." She looked at him instead of at her teacup then. There was so much hope on her face that he was really glad he could help her out with this. "You're not able to have any illnesses. That would include anything that might well have been passed down to you. The reason I know this is because when I was younger, I asked one of my aunts if the possibility of having gene pool issues would be a problem for an animal as big as we are. As in, what if a mate was ill with something like you're talking about, how would it affect a dragon. She told me it wouldn't be there. That essentially, when you were given the ability to live forever, you'd be free of anything like that, along with cancer and other long-term illnesses. You'd have nothing in your DNA that would produce a child with a handicap."

"Will you and Pem have children?" He told her they were working on figuring that out. "Because you're a dragon, and she's not. I would imagine that her having an egg would be difficult since she isn't built for that."

"My brothers and I are the first generation of dragons that were born to dragons that were turned into human shifters." He explained to her that his father was a dragon when he'd been born and changed to shift into a human when he was just a young dragon. "So, in answer to your question, I don't know if we'll be able to have any. You and Milo would be able to if he's your mate. You're neither one dragons, so we're betting that the possibility of you having a child would be better than with me having one with Pem."

"Because of the dragon thing." He laughed and told her that was it. "I don't know if I'm his mate. I don't know what to think about him being the one either. I'm just getting my life together and figuring out what I can do. I'm not saying that I'd turn him down. I mean, just hanging around you guys, I know there isn't anyone better than the Manning men."

"Thank you for that. I'll pass that on to my parents. They'll be happy to know they did a good job of raising us." Theo sipped his tea. He didn't push her into whatever else she wanted to talk about but let her work it out. Looking around the kitchen, he realized that she was doing for herself. There was no cook here. No staff that he'd come across. He wondered if she had not hired them because of her need to have things quiet or just hadn't gotten around to it. Theo started to ask her about it when she spoke again.

"I've noticed that you don't tell Pem what to do. Do you suppose that if Milo is my mate, he'll do the same thing?" Theo told her he thought she could put him in his place if he did start that. "Yes, I suppose I would. I'm not much of a people person. I'm all right once I get to know you, but I'm not the sort of person that goes out much and parties. I prefer a good book over the television. Working in the yard instead of being in the house. Also, I enjoy just being out of doors. I'm not sure how that is going to work either."

"It'll work because the fates have chosen you if you are above all other women in the world to match up perfectly with your mate. Milo, for the most part, would rather stay home than to date. All of us enjoy the outdoors. I think a lot of that stems from being a creature of the earth. George and Milo are not dragons, but they are powerful beings. They get their magic the same as us, from all the elements that make magic for the world."

The two of them spoke for several more minutes before George joined them. He opened her fridge and closed it. When he opened it the second time, he could see that it had been filled. Taking out the stuff to make subs, George told them what he knew.

"First of all, I want to let you know that your fridge is magical. I believe all of ours are, and there isn't any reason for you to do without. Whatever you want will appear in it. Including juice, which, no matter if Milo is your mate or not, you'll need to drink more of. Magic is draining." He set a thick roast beef sub in front of Theo and a meatball one in front of Jamie. "Milo is resting now. No longer in the deep sleep he'd been in. Just having the iron taken from his body is making him feel a great deal better. I've not bothered talking to Winnie. She'll let us know when she knows what happened."

Again, they talked for a while. Pem joined them when they moved to the parlor. After a while, the rest of the family showed up, each of them checking on Milo to see if he was all right. Mom and Dad had been informed and said they would be there soon. He felt terrible that they'd been here so much. Maybe they'd move here soon. That would be great.

Supper was ordered when it became apparent that no one wanted to leave just yet. Jamie, for all her liking quiet time, was doing well with all of them there. He hoped that Milo was her mate. It would be epic to have them together.

~*~

Milo didn't move around too much. It wasn't that he couldn't, but he was achy. He'd never experienced anything like this before. Lily had brought him some clothing from his house, and he had thought about taking a shower. Even the thought of getting out of the bed again after going to the bathroom made him want to nap again. Lily asked him if he was all right.

"I'm sure I am. I just feel like I've been run over. I never understood that saying before today. Christ, I do feel like exactly that has been done to me." Lily laid her head on his forehead and told him he was no longer as hot. "Good. That means I'm not feverish anymore."

That had startled him, having a fever. Even as a child, he'd never been sick. Never had anything close to a fever. Nor had he fought a cold. He thought this was the reason he felt so sore. It had never happened to him before.

The lady of the house hadn't been to see him since he'd woken up. His brothers had. So had Rachel and Pem. He'd thought she was avoiding him, but Lily assured him that she was very busy taking a test. It had taken him asking his brothers what sort of test would take so much time, and it turned out she was simply studying for her board exams, not just taking a test.

"She's going to work in the hospital. Run the entire surgery department for us." He asked Theo if Pem was going to work there as well. "I've not asked her directly, but I think that is her plan. The two of them together have been making adjustments to the plans that even the architect is impressed with. Also, you'll be glad to know it'll be easier going green with this project. Solar panels are going to be on most of the roof, as well as one-quarter of the back lot. Having all that land is going to save a great deal of money in the way of heating and cooling."

Milo told Theo about the things he'd been able to unearth where he'd been. Getting in and out of computers had always been something he'd been very good at.

Apparently, in the office they ran—it took care of their massive amounts of donations—the computers had been bogged down with not just games, but movies and personal information that was slowing the computers to the point of them not running as well as they all knew they should have been.

"The program I designed will not only keep them from using the computers for anything personal but now that they have to log in and out of the Internet with their cards, it will make sure they're working when they should be. I was amazed to find out that almost sixty percent of their time was spent on shopping and browsing the Internet. No wonder it takes them so long to get back to us on payroll questions."

Theo had come to see him a couple of times today, earlier that morning and then just a few minutes after he'd gotten his clothing from Lily. Milo was worried he was taking Theo from whatever he had been doing, but his brother assured him that Pem was studying too, and he was bored. He wasn't sure how to take himself being a replacement for boredom, but he didn't comment.

"I wanted to see how you were feeling now. I know I was here only a couple of hours ago, but there are some things I'd like you to help me out with. Just questions mostly, but I could use your input on them." Milo sat up straighter in the bed and felt better for it. "Also, you should know that I've spoken to Jamie. She's been in and out of here while you were sleeping. She's going to come and see you later tonight. But she really is working hard."

"You guys still think she's my mate?" Theo said he didn't think she was. "Why is that? I mean, don't you want me to have a beautiful wife too?"

"Nah, nothing like that. But she's been here with you, in and out, and neither of you seems to be foaming at the mouth to be together." That made him laugh, and he was sure that was what Theo was intending for him to do. "Not only that, but she's more like you than I thought. Quiet and reserved. She doesn't even own a television. Not that it's a deal breaker, but she seems to just not care what is going on in the world around her. I think she's always been that way. I keep getting sidetracked when I go to ask Pem about her."

"I bet you do."

They laughed again when someone knocked at the door. Milo pulled the covers up over his bare chest when he bid the person entry. He'd bet anything that the woman standing there was Jamie.

"Hello."

Before You Go...

HELP AN AUTHOR

write a review

THANK YOU!

Share your voice and help guide other readers to these wonderful books. Even if it's only a line or two, your reviews help readers discover the author's books so they can continue creating stories that you'll love. Login to your favorite retailer and leave a review. Thank you.

AWARD WINNING, BESTSELLING AUTHOR

Kathi Barton, a winner of the Pinnacle Book Achievement Award and a best-selling author on Amazon and All Romance books, lives in Nashport, Ohio, with her husband, Paul. When not creating new worlds and romance, Kathi and her husband enjoy camping and going to auctions. She can also be seen at county fairs with her husband, who is an artist and potter.

Her muse, a cross between Jimmy Stewart and Hugh Jackman, brings her stories to life for her readers in a way that has them coming back time and again for more. Her favorite genre is paranormal romance, with a great deal of spice. You can visit Kathi online and drop her an email if you'd like. She loves hearing from her fans. aaronskiss@gmail.com.

Follow Kathi on her blog: http://kathisbartonauthor. blogspot.com/

www.ingramcontent.com/pod-product-compliance
Lightning Source LLC
Chambersburg PA
CBHW061230170626
46809CB00007B/2592